Caught Up in a D-Boy's Illest Love
TN Jones

Caught Up in a D-Boy's Illest Love

Acknowledgments

First, thanks must go out to the Higher Being for providing me with a sound body and mind; in addition to having the natural talent of writing and blessing me with the ability to tap into such an amazing part of life. Second, thanks most definitely go out to my Princess. Third, to my supporters and new readers for giving me a chance. Where in the world would I be without y'all?

Truth be told, I wouldn't have made it this far without anyone. I truly thank everyone for rocking with me. MUAH! Y'all make this writing journey enjoyable! I would like to thank everyone from the bottom of my heart for always rocking with the novelist kid from Alabama, no matter what I drop. Y'all have once again trusted me to provide y'all with quality entertainment.

Enjoy, my loves!

Caught Up in a D-Boy's Illest Love

TN Jones: Casey and Jonsey, thank you for taking the time to sit down with me.

Jonsey: (Looks nervous as she fumbles with her fingers) You are welcome.

Casey: (Staring at Jonsey) You are welcome.

TN Jones: So, Jonsey, tell us a little bit about yourself.

Jonsey: Um, okay. I'm Jonsey Brown. I'm twenty-three. I'm the fourth of five children; my family says I'm the quietest out of the bunch. I attend Alabama State University; I'm getting a Bachelor's degree in Business Management. I love to fish, watch TV, shop, bake, and cook. Basically, I'm just a below-average Joe.

TN Jones: Jonsey, how long have you known him?

Jonsey: I have seen him around my neighborhood for three years. We frequented the same store, but I truly didn't get to know him until some months ago.

TN Jones: How does he makes you feel?

Jonsey: At times, he fucking disgusts me, and the other times I'm absolutely smitten with him.

TN Jones: Do you regret meeting him?

Jonsey: I think so, but I'm not quite sure.

Casey: How do you not know if you regret meeting me, Ms. Lady?

Caught Up in a D-Boy's Illest Love

(She doesn't answer him as she gathers her things and exits the interview room)

TN Jones: Casey, I guess it's me and you now. Tell me a little bit about yourself.

Casey: I'm twenty-nine years old, no children, and self-employed. Have a Bachelor's degree in Engineering. I'm the only child. Love to enjoy life.

TN Jones: How do you feel about Jonsey?

Casey: She's sweet, smart, and down to earth in a shy way. A brother got feelings for her.

TN Jones: What happened between the two of y'all?

Casey: (phone rings, look down at it) Mane, all I can say is read our book. Just BS and chaos are what happened between the two of us.

TN Jones: Are you going to try and work at a friendship at least?

Casey: Nope. I'm going to work at her forgiving and marrying me.

Jonsey: (storms in angrily) How in the fuck is that going to happen, Casey?

TN Jones: Flip the page and indulge yourself into their story as it's told by them.

Chapter 1
Casey aka Dank

Friday, December 2nd, 2016

What I thought would be a smooth transaction between Baymatch and I turned out to be a drawn-out play. It's the same shit that I grew tired of dealing with every other week—him trying to put me and my partner on his hustling team. Staring at the tall, husky, pimp-like meth dealer, my face was blank as I knew he was going to ask me the same questions that he did last week and the weeks prior to that.

"Would you like to be on the team, Dank?" he inquired as he leaned back on the large, leather sofa.

"Nawl, I'm good Baymatch," I replied casually as I gave him full eye contact.

Sighing heavily, he asked smoothly in a deep baritone timbre, "You sure you don't need any runners, Dank?"

"Hell yeah I'm sure. Totta and I can move by ourselves. The less people in our way the better," I voiced seriously as I gulped the cold, brown liquor.

"Well, let me rephrase. Would you like to join *my* team?" he inquired putting emphasis on the word my.

Caught Up in a D-Boy's Illest Love

Glaring into the face of the light-skinned, mediocre dope boy, I sternly replied, "For the one-hundredth time, no. I prefer to keep buying work from you. I prefer a two-man team. I'm sure you understand."

"But you don't have the connects that you need when solo dolo," he pressed, annoying the hell out of me with his antics of trying to recruit me.

Shaking my head as I held his gaze, I swirled the small glass that held a swallow of Hennessey. Knowing that Baymatch was going to try his best to recruit me, I sat back and waited for him to continue speaking.

"All I'm saying is that you would do great under my wing, Dank. You would be protected by the most notorious street group, The Savage Clique. I have added more men to my roster, followed by linking underneath The Savage Clique," he informed me as he put a Cuban cigar to his mouth.

Nodding my head at what he was saying, I knew about The Savage Clique. It was owned and heavily operated by a broad named X. I've heard around town and other cities how tight her team was. I knew without a doubt that I didn't want to be involved with them; they were into all types of shit. Truth be told, I just wanted to lay low and make a little money and not the type of money that she and everyone else in The Savage Clique made. Basically, I just wanted some low-key money. I wasn't trying to take over the city or the country. Being in the streets was more of a stress reliever of mine, so a brother didn't need that unwanted attention.

"There are so many perks to being a part of my team," he continued as he kept his eyes on me.

Growing extremely pissed off, I shook my head while chuckling. It took everything in me not to spaz out on his ass. Doing breathing exercises, I said, "Baymatch, you know I fucks with you the long way, right?"

"I do," he replied as he lit a cigar keeping his hazel-greenish eyes on me.

"I don't mean no harm when I say I'd rather be on a two-man team. Less people know my business the better. I cop dope from you because you have quality shit. So, our business is over once I pay you for what I want."

Nodding his head with a smirk on his face, Baymatch leaned towards me, licked his lips, and awkwardly responded, "What Baymatch wants, he gets. I hope you understand that."

Thrown off by his behavior, I chuckled, shook my head, and stared at him as if he lost his mind. *I know damn well this nigga ain't on that funny shit,* I thought as I twirled the glass on my knee. *Let me get the fuck out of here. This is going to be my last time coming to cop dope from this nigga,* I thought as I stood up, feeling uncomfortable.

"It was nice conducting business with you, mane. I'mma holla at cha," I informed him as I placed the glass on the dusty, circular table.

"Everyone loves Baymatch," he quickly responded as he stood up before coming closer to me.

Without a moment's hesitation, I pulled out my Glock and pressed it to the fuckboy's forehead.

"Are you on that fuck boy shit?" I growled, eager to splatter his dome.

Laughing, Baymatch stared into my eyes. Immediately, I became pissed that he didn't answer my question; therefore, I yelled, "Are you on that fuckboy shit?"

"I wouldn't call it fuckboy shit. I would call it a blessing from the other side."

"Well, I don't want *that* blessing from the other side, my nigga," I angrily growled as Baymatch's front door slowly opened.

Not knowing who was going to be on the other side of the door, panic set in. I didn't know if there was going to be a battle for my life or not. I knew that I wasn't going to go out without a fight; therefore, I quickly snatched Baymatch closer to me with my iron pressed against the side of his neck. I was going to make sure that everything turned out in my favor.

It was a blessing that my cousin, Colt, was the one that strolled through Baymatch's door. Then the thoughts hit me. *Why in the fuck is Colt walking through Baymatch's door as if he lived here? Did he have a key? Did he knock on the door?*

"Whoa. Dank, put the gun down. What's the problem?" Colt's high-pitched voice asked me as his eyes stayed on Baymatch.

A weird feeling settled in the pit of my stomach upon seeing the grim, scared look on my baby cousin's face. I had to snap out of the trance that Colt's facial expression had on me.

"This nigga tried to come on to me," I quickly announced as Baymatch chuckled before speaking.

"Colt, tell your cousin how loving I can be. How gentle I am when I'm pleas—," Baymatch began to say before two bullets graced his face.

Blood and brain matter splattered over me as my eyes never left the drug dealer's body. As I glared at

Caught Up in a D-Boy's Illest Love

Baymatch's dead body, my mind was rehashing what he said to my cousin and what he was implying. Not one time did I give a fuck about his DNA being near my mouth, eyes, and nose.

Was this nigga fucking my cousin or raping him? How long was this shit going on? Who else's backdoor was this nigga blessing? I thought at the same time Colt angrily spat, "The streets better without that fuck nigga present."

Completely stuck in place, there wasn't a sound that left my mouth. I was in shock of what I heard. All I could do was think to myself on when and how things transpired between them. Colt began to stutter some words as he tucked his gun into the back of his pants.

Needing to make sense of everything, I placed my eyes on my tall, lean cousin before asking, "Was that nigga raping you?"

Ignoring my question, Colt waltzed back and forth talking amongst himself. After fifteen minutes of watching him, I placed my gun in the holster, followed by retrieving my mobile device. With my phone in my hand, I held down on the number three button and patiently waited for it to ring. It seemed like it took forever for my partner of twenty years, Totta, to answer.

Shortly after the sixth ring, his deep, baritone voice said, "What up?"

"We got a problem," I quickly spoke.

"Where?"

Not wanting him to pull up at Baymatch's crib, I began to think on where he needed to come. Silence overtook the phone as I thought of a way for him to come into Baymatch's crib.

All Totta heard me say was, "Uhh, uhh."

"Where, nigga!" Totta said loudly.

"I shoulda been murked that wicked, nasty ass nigga the first time he touched me!" Colt yelled before slumping onto the ground.

"What the fuck did Colt just say and why? Where the fuck you at, mane?"

I couldn't answer for staring at my confused cousin. His body language told me that he was distraught and on the verge of rehashing the unwanted private time with Baymatch.

"Dank, where the fuck you at, man?" Totta inquired sternly.

Caught Up in a D-Boy's Illest Love

"Baymatch's," I heard myself say as my eyes were glued on Colt.

"Ah, fuck! Shit, fuck. I'm on the way. Don't do shit until I get there," he demanded as I heard shuffling in the background.

"A'ight," I replied as I shook my head.

Soon as I hung up the phone, I tried to talk to my cousin. However, he was in a world of his own. Immediately, I felt bad for him. Colton Mosley, aka Colt, wasn't a street type of dude even though he liked to be seen in the streets. Truth be told, my cousin wasn't cut out for the streets. He was the do-boy to the higher-ranking street guys such as Baymatch. Colt would shoot but only when he was scared. Totta referred to him as a scary shooter; the ones that will shoot a gun with their eyes closed.

"Colt, talk to me," I voiced in a low tone as I looked at him.

"Leave, I'll clean this mess up," he replied as he pulled his gun out of his back pocket.

"Nawl, Totta on his way over here to help me clean this up. I want you to leave, now."

"You ain't finna get caught up in my mess; Auntie Geraldine would have a fit. I shot him, and I'm going to take the rap for it," he responded as tears streamed down his face.

"Dank, I'm no punk. I'm no punk, cuz."

"I'm not worried about any of that shit, Colt," I replied as I hopped off the sofa and quickly moved towards my cousin, who was against the wall on the verge of breaking down.

When I was within arm's reach, I pulled him closer to me as I comforted him.

"Colt, I need you to leave now. I got this. Go home and don't say shit to nobody, understand?" I whispered in his ear at the same time we heard a window breaking in the kitchen area.

We pulled away from each other and placed our hands on our weapons when we heard Totta say in a low tone, "It's Totta, Dank."

Relaxing my arm, I replied, "Come in the front room."

Totta's six foot two, dark-skinned, athletic body waltzed into the murder scene with an 'oh shit' facial expression. Immediately, he placed his eyes on a distraught Colt. He was about to open his mouth to say something to him, but I shook my head before saying, "Not now, Totta."

Caught Up in a D-Boy's Illest Love

Nodding his head, Totta threw us a pair of black gloves and a thin, blue hair net. Colt looked at the hair net in a confused manner, which prompted me to tell him, "Put them over your shoes." Nodding his head, we began to put the items in their respectful places.

Soon as we were finished, Totta asked me, "Where are your keys?"

"Why?"

"Because I have some niggas outside that's finna come and get your car. We will leave out the back. The street is filled with people, and the last thing you want is for them to see you and Colt leaving here. At least this will buy us some time to get shit under wraps, feel me?"

"Yeah," I voiced as I threw him my keys.

Upon catching them, Totta was out the same way he came. When he returned, we began to clean up the crime scene. While tiptoeing through the front room, we heard voices in the front yard. My heart was racing a mile a minute as I didn't know what to expect. Coming to a complete stop, I analyzed the voices as they talked.

"Shit, Baymatch got the best dope in the city, Kev," a squeaky voiced individual stated as he came closer to the front door.

"You think he gonna credit us some of that quality dope?" the other person inquired before knocking on the unlocked door.

Colt slowly moved towards the door and carefully locked it without making a sound.

Knock. Knock. Knock.

I held my breath as I didn't want to make a sound. Colt was shaking like a stripper on a Tuesday night. Totta was firing up a cigarette as he had an 'I don't give a fuck' expression across his face. Several more knocks sounded off before the individuals left. Exhaling heavily, I glanced at Totta, who brought his head forward— once.

That was our cue to finish the task at hand. It didn't take us long to wipe down everything in the front room, retrieve two shell casings, and to mop the floors. As we were close to finishing things up, Totta stated, "Two of my mechanic guys finna pull up and act like something is wrong with your whip. Upon the slamming of the hood, they are going to tow your car to their shop. The slamming of your hood is the cue for us to get the fuck out of here. Understand?"

"Yeah," I replied strongly at the same time Colt said, "What about the cameras?"

Caught Up in a D-Boy's Illest Love

With a stunned look on my face, Totta replied, "Where in the fuck are they?"

"Everywhere. The main setup is in his closet."

Motioning his head for Colt to follow him, Totta aimed for the long, lightly lit hallway. In four minutes of them being gone, the hood of my car was slammed. Growing antsy, I was ready to flee. Without a clue as to what I was supposed to be doing, I fled down the hallway to assist those niggas in getting rid of the video feed.

One thing I knew for certain was that I didn't want anyone to see us; however, that was going to be impossible giving it was two o'clock in the fucking afternoon. There weren't any houses in the back of Baymatch's crib, but there were homes in the front and sides of his crib. Totta clearly stated that we were to go out of the back window and flee down the alleyway behind the deceased dope boy's home.

Forty-five minutes later, we were out the back window with a medium-sized duffel bag of dope, money, and the entire video camera system—motherfucking cords and all. Totta was the last one to slide through the window. When he sped past us, I knew that I had to run like hell, which prompted Colt to run also. Wanting to look back, I didn't; I simply kept running until we had to jump a fence. Once we were over the fence, we saw Totta's silver Yukon truck parked in the dirty alley with the hood up. Quickly walking towards Totta's ducked off whip, I was a nervous mess. I had to tell myself several times to calm down. Normally, it worked, but today that shit didn't!

"Y'all gotta explain shit to me, pronto," Totta informed us after he shut the hood of his whip.

"Get us the fuck out of this area," I replied as I slumped down in the front seat.

"Baymatch has been doing sexual things to me for the past three years. I tried my damnedest to tell him that I wasn't like that, but he insisted that it take place or that I would die," Colt's trembling voice stated at the same time my heart broke at the thought of him enduring such humility.

"Colt, mane, Colt," Totta said as he shook his head and started the engine on his whip.

There wasn't anything that anyone could say behind what we learned. Never in a million years would I have thought that Baymatch was doing unspeakable things to my cousin. I was glad that he was no longer living. Niggas like that made me sick to my stomach. I knew without a doubt that Baymatch was going to rot in hell for what he did to my family member. If Colt was being raped by the fuck nigga, I knew that there was plenty more niggas in the street being done the same way.

***

When I woke up, I didn't know that I would've had one helluva day. If I had of known, I would've turned off my cell phone and never left the damn house. What started out as a beautiful, sunny, warm winter day turned into a cold, gruesome, bone-chilling type of day and night.

Ever since we left Baymatch's crib, nothing was right. Colt was quiet and to himself. Totta and I couldn't stop talking about the things that Baymatch could've done to my cousin. It got to a point where I was ready to forget the entire day, but I couldn't. How could anyone forget the look on their family member's face after such humility was brought out of the closet?

"Mane, we need to go out tonight?" Totta stated, interrupting my thoughts.

"Shit, I agree. Sitting in this crib is driving me insane. I can't take the quietness from Colt. I can't take the images of how disturbed he was before you arrived. I need six drinks and to get my dick sucked. I need my mind far off the shit that was revealed today," I voiced lightly as I began to roll me a blunt.

"I second that motion. So, what club are we hitting up tonight?"

"I guess Club Freeze."

Ring. Ring. Ring.

Glancing at my phone, which was sitting in my lap, I saw Trasheeda's name displaying across the screen. With a smirk on my face, I thought, *She's the type of freak that I need in my life right now.*

On the fourth ring, I said, "Yo."

"What are you doing?"

"Shit, in need of busting a nut or two. Let me slide through."

As she replied, "Come on," Totta was chuckling as he shook his head and pulled out his cell phone.

"I'll be there in ten minutes."

"Bet," she replied before hanging up the phone.

"Don't get caught up in that freak's shit, Dank," my partner warned in a joking manner.

"Now, woe, you know that'll never be my move. Can't no bitch get me caught up. I'm done with that love shit," I told him as I stood up and dusted the small crumbs of weed off my jeans.

Caught Up in a D-Boy's Illest Love

"So you say," he replied sarcastically.

"Aye, Colt, I'm finna step out for a minute. Call me if you need me," I stated in a loud manner.

"A'ight," I heard him say from the living room.

Ring. Ring. Ring.

"Aye, Totta, if you happen to leave before I get back...lock my crib up and make sure that Colt is okay before you leave," I commanded him as I held out my hand to dap him up.

Nodding his head, he answered his phone.

"Speak to me," he demanded.

On the way out of the door, he said, "Shit, keep me informed at all costs," which made me come to a complete stop.

Looking back at him, he voiced, "Baymatch's mother found his body. Police are all through his shit."

"Well, let's hope that we handled our shit the right way. Call me if you need me. I'll be back once I'm done busting these nuts," I voiced nonchalantly before walking out of the door.

God, watch over my cousin, Totta, and me, I prayed as I breathed in the humid night's air as I was in need of diving into some pussy.

Chapter 2
Jonsey

I was soaking in the tub after a long day of working. A variety of songs by Mary J. Blige played from my music app on my phone. I had my entire evening and night planned out—doing absolutely nothing but binge watching the television show *Gotham*.

Bam. Bam. Bam.

Who is knocking on my door like that? I thought as I sat upright in the tub.

Bam. Bam. Bam.

I sighed heavily as I was rushed away from my relaxing bath.

I know Jonzella didn't leave her keys, so who's knocking at the door like that? I thought as I carefully hopped out of the tub at the same time I reached for my freshly scented, white, cotton robe.

"Who is it?" I yelled as I opened the bathroom door. By the silly gestures the people made at my door, I knew who it was—my immature brothers, Kevin and Kenny.

"Kenny and Kevin. Open up, sis," my brothers replied in unison while playfully beating on the door.

Caught Up in a D-Boy's Illest Love

"Why are y'all playing on the door like that? What are y'all doing here?" I asked the knuckleheads before opening the door.

"Dang. We can't come by to see what our baby sisters are up to?" Kenny voiced casually as he waltzed in, aiming for the refrigerator.

"Hmm, hmm, I bet that is what y'all came here for," I replied with my hands on my hips after I closed and locked the door.

Kevin took a seat on the long sofa as he snatched the remote control off the seat cushion. They engaged in small talk as I stared at them without saying a word. I observed their beings as if I didn't grow up with them under the same roof. Kevin was twenty-five years old, stood about five feet eight, and was skinny as hell. His medium-brown, long-shaped face was complemented by his medium-beaded, brown eyes. Kevin's left arm was filled with tattoos, which my mother cursed him out for weeks behind his actions.

Kenneth, aka Kenny, was twenty-seven years old, stood around five feet nine, lean, medium-brown skin, and had large beaded, brown eyes. Both had thick eyebrows, big noses, and a beautiful smile. My parents said that they were dropped on their heads when they were younger. That's why they can't grasp what they need to do as adult men; I truly believed my parents.

"Jonsey, where's Jonzella?" Kenny asked, interrupting my thoughts.

"Uh, gone to the store," I replied as I stood at the door, looking at them like they were crazy.

"You can go shower, stinky butt," Kevin said as he plopped on the sofa beside Kenny with a bowl of cereal.

"Um, why are y'all here?" I inquired again with my hands on my hips.

"Because we want to be. Do we always have to have a reason to hang out with our sisters?" Kenny asked, glaring into my eyes.

"N-no," I stammered, looking down at the ground as I fumbled with my hands.

My brothers burst out in laughter before Kenny announced, "You gots to be shitting me, Jonsey. How in the hell are you still shy with brothers like us and a sister like Jonzella?"

"We have gone over this several times, y'all. Just because we are sisters and brothers don't mean that we must have the same characteristics. Ugh, y'all work my nerves," I voiced in an agitated tone while rolling my eyes.

Caught Up in a D-Boy's Illest Love

"You gotta break out of that, sis," Kenny replied seriously.

"I know," I responded as I began to exit the living room, aiming for the bathroom.

Ever since I could remember, I always felt weird whenever someone looked me in my eyes. I guess I thought they would be able to see my insecurities and read my thoughts. Eye contact was my main problem; I could look someone in their eyes briefly, but long eye contact always made me nervous.

Slipping into the lukewarm water, I turned on the hot water knob. Grabbing my green washcloth, I began to bathe my body. As Mary J. Blige sang "Not Gon' Cry", I tuned in with the R&B singer and sang my butt off, all the while cleaning my body.

Soon as I drained the water out of the tub, my cell phone rang. Scooping it into my wrinkled hand, I answered the call from my sister.

"Hello," I announced casually as I dried my body off.

"Let's go out tonight," her high-pitched tone stated as the background noise grew louder.

"Okay. Where to?"

"Club Freeze."

"Okay. What's the dress attire?"

Caught Up in a D-Boy's Illest Love

Laughing before responding, my sister said, "Um, why does everything have to be coordinated?"

"Because I'm a perfectionist, you know that," I chuckled as I strolled towards the cabinet that held the cleaning products.

"Anything that is sexy. It's a black and white affair tonight. So, grab something that's black or white and extremely sexy. Make sure you shave your hairy ass legs, arms, and underarms," she spat before laughing.

Snickering, I replied, "Bye, heifer."

I really didn't want to go to a club; I preferred to stay at home and watch the latest season of *Gotham*. I was a homebody, and I liked that. I wasn't the type to be in a club every weekend; I was the type to stay at home, study, and be peaceful. True enough, I was a young adult, but I didn't like to be around a large crowd of people as most young adults liked.

I never smoked weed, but I did drink. I didn't smoke cigarettes or Black-N-Milds. I wasn't the type to be all in a guy or guys face; hell, half of the time I was liable to pass out if they looked me in my eyes too long. Don't get me wrong, I wasn't the type to pass up a conversation with anyone. If it didn't involve anyone trying to get to know me on a personal level, then I was fine.

Caught Up in a D-Boy's Illest Love

Conversing with my coworkers was a piece of cake—we worked while talking, useless chatter basically.

Simply put, my nature was overall shy until I got to know you better. People were the main reason that I stayed to myself. They could be so judgmental and spiteful, and truth be told, I didn't have time for it. I had my feelings hurt one too many times by people that claimed to be my friends. Thus, resulting in me not having any female friends, just associates from work and school. I always picked the wrong crowd to be around, which resulted in me getting in trouble at home. Seeing that my choosing of friends was off, I decided that it was best to just hang solely with my best friend turned sister, Jonzella.

"Sis!" Kenny yelled from the top of the hallway, interrupting my thoughts.

"What?"

"Can we crash here with y'all tonight?" he asked.

"If Jonzella is cool with it, then so am I," I lied.

Let me text her ass right now that they can't stay here, I thought as I opened the text message thread between her and me.

"She said it's cool," Kenny voiced casually.

"Shit," I mumbled as I pressed the send button.

"A'ight," I replied as I opened the bathroom door.

Extremely not in the mood to deal with my annoying ass brothers, I strolled into my room to find my attire for the night. In three minutes, I found the perfect outfit. Plopping down on the bed, I heard Jonzella speaking to our brothers.

"Are y'all going out with me and Jonsey, tonight?"

"Where y'all going?" I heard Kevin inquire.

"Club Freeze."

"Hell yes. We need to find something to wear," I heard Kenny respond.

"Are we hitting up the mall or what?" Jonzella asked them.

The entire time they talked, I wanted to know why in the hell they were staying over here versus the house they were living at with some friends of theirs. I didn't want them invading our space or causing any problems for Jonzella and me. The last thing I needed was for them to have folks kicking in the door for some stupid shit they did.

***

At eleven o'clock p.m., we strolled through the VIP line at Club Freeze. It was a packed house tonight, and immediately, I felt as if I was going to have a panic attack. All emotions calmed down soon as Kenny handed me my favorite mixed drink: Seven Deadly Sins. After he handed me my drink, he stated, "Kevin and I are going to stroll around the club. Have fun, sis. Let your hair down. You are always so uptight. If y'all have any trouble, come get us."

Yes, our brothers were troublemakers; however, I can honestly say that they didn't allow any guys to use us or hurt our feelings. They didn't play the radio when it came down to worthless guys and us.

"Okay," I replied as the beat of one of Future's songs blared from the speakers, causing me to move along to the beat while bobbing my head.

Kenny whispered something in Jonzella's ear, which required her to nod her head. Ten times out of ten he told her the same thing he told me. Soon as our brothers were out of eyesight, we slowly strolled through the sea of people standing in front of the bar.

With my black shades over my face, I saw quite a few eye candies in the building. Dark chocolate to light-skinned males were all over the place. Some dressed to impress while others should've stayed their bum asses at home. Women that were fully dressed to half-naked were either on the stage, dance floor, or clung to the arms of the men.

"Excuse me," I stated to a group of females before saying those words again to a group of four males.

As I said a thousand excuse me's, at the end of the bar, my eyes fell on one individual that always took my breath away. The one person that made numerous butterflies appear in my stomach, made my hands tremble, and breathing become erratic—Eleven Golds, as I called him.

He received that nickname because he had that many in his mouth—six at the top and five at the bottom. His five feet six, lean frame was dressed in a money green collared shirt, denim jeans, which had a money green belt in the loops, and money green, dark blue, and white Jordan's on his feet. One golden nugget was in his right ear, a thick gold bracelet was on his right wrist, and a gold watch on his left wrist. The gold on his body highlighted his chocolatey skin; the brother was fine! He was a sight for sore eyes.

I stood still as I watched him run his hand across his growing beard. His jet black, low haircut was seeking for my hands to run across the massive waves it held.

Caught Up in a D-Boy's Illest Love

He had juicy lips that he licked with his thick, long tongue.

My God. I wonder what those feel like, I thought as I felt hands pushing me forward.

Halfway towards our destination, I felt myself becoming shy at the thought of him and me conversing longer than three minutes. Thus, I gave myself a pep talk.

Nih, bitch, you said the next time you saw him you weren't going to clam up. You are a grown ass woman, so act like it, my inner voice spat as I rapidly rushed away from Eleven Golds and his crew.

"Are you clamming up?" Jonzella yelled in my ear.

Shaking my head, I snapped out of the trance he had me in.

"Got that liquid courage in my system remember," I said as I shook the large, plastic cup.

"Good. Maybe you will finally ask the man his name and be able to carry on a conversation with him," she stated as she motioned for me to step onto the dance floor.

Shaking my head, I stepped to the side—informing her to take the lead. Once in front of me, she did just that as the DJ played "Throw This Money" by USDA. That was Jonzella's song, and I knew she was going to cut up.

"Ohh, shit!" she screamed as she held up her right hand and bounced her butt.

With my cup in my hand, I brought it to my lips and swallowed the rest of the contents. My insides became warm; thus, waking up the 'I don't give a fuck' attitude. Between the liquor, seeing Jonzella having fun on the dance floor, and the song, I loosened up and joined her on the dance floor. I started doing the dance that my mother hates so much, I bent over and let my ass cheeks do numbers—up, down, up, down, followed by one cheek, and then two cheeks. The killer move came in when I started making them clap; first slowly, and then rapidly. That's when I felt someone behind me. Not caring, I continued to twerk. The twerking song ended and was replaced with a slow, rap sex song.

If the females didn't go crazy over USDA's song, they surely did once the unknown artist of the slow song played. I surely was one of those females that went crazy but in a good way. I wasn't with the hollering and jumping up and down; I simply let my body flow along with the seductive beat.

Caught Up in a D-Boy's Illest Love

The singing females winded their bodies slow as the males quickly jumped behind them. With my unknown male dancer behind me, I rolled my behind on him. Quickly feeling his member rise, I had to gasp because whoever was behind me had a dick on them. Wanting to know how long it was, I touched my ankles and slowly dragged my ass down until I found where it stopped it—the middle of his thigh!

My fucking goodness. Who got a dick like that? I thought as I turned my head to see.

Not knowing exactly what to do when my eyes landed on Eleven Golds, I did the safest thing—continued to dance. Rotating my hips along with the song, he began to pull me towards him.

With my back on his strong chest, his deep timbre stated seductively, "So, you are finally outside after dark."

Even though I nodded my head, I mouthed yes. I was waiting on the day for him or me to approach one another without me being shy, and now here we were, and I was somewhat cooler than a fan on a fall night— letting things work themselves out for the two of us.

"Turn around so that I can talk to you, Ms. Lady," he commanded gently.

Caught Up in a D-Boy's Illest Love

Instantly, I felt like we were the only two in the club. Turning around to look at him, I wasn't shy or nervous; I was relaxed, and I thanked God for that. Soon as our eyes connected, I tuned out the blasting music and those around us. There were no shaking hands, no butterflies trapped in my stomach, and no voices saying that I wasn't good enough. Moments like this I cherished because I was so self-conscious of myself. I could carry a conversation without worrying about what others thought of me, or mainly what I thought of myself.

"For starters, we must know each other's name," he voiced while smiling as he pushed my shades on top of my head.

Nodding my head with a light chuckle, I replied, "Indeed. I'm Jonsey."

This man is fucking fine. He is of the best genes, I thought as I glared into his brown peepers.

"Hmm, that's a unique name. I'm Casey," he voiced as he extended his left hand.

Placing my hand into his, I couldn't stop my thoughts from imagining his firm, soft hands roaming over my body.

"It's a pleasure to know your name and see you less shy," he sounded off as we shook hands.

"Likewise."

"In Town" by 2Chainz slowed the twerking crowd down, which prompted Casey to slide his body closer to mine. Slow dancing to the beat, we conversed. As I enjoyed his conversation, I noticed Jonzella was face-to-face with a tall, dark-skinned brother; she was grinning all in the dude's face.

I will be having full details about that guy, I thought as Casey asked me, "So, how old are you?"

"Twenty-three and you?"

"Twenty-nine."

"Any girlfriends?" I inquired with a raised eyebrow.

"No. Any boyfriends or girlfriends?"

"No to both questions," I chuckled lightly.

"Hmm," he replied while looking down at me.

"What does that mean?" I asked with a smirk on my face.

"Nothing, Ms. Lady," he voiced as he showed his eleven golds.

Grinning, I shook my head. It seemed as if time had stopped as well as the music. I couldn't say anything for the joy that I was feeling.

Caught Up in a D-Boy's Illest Love

Smiling like a Cheshire cat, I was. Feeling myself, I was. Ready to drop my draws, shit I was! I awaited this for a while with my scary, shy tail.

"I see now that you gon' make a nigga hold you hostage."

"Let me know it's real then," my somewhat cocky ass stated.

Laughing, he dropped his mouth to my ear. "Yo' ass been drinking, huh? You too bold tonight. Any other time, you will speak, hold a light conversation, and be on about your business."

"Thank the Seven Deadly Sins drink for that."

"Then I must thank the drink that has you able to converse with me."

With a pleasant smile, I nodded my head. If it wasn't for the drink, I would've been still dreaming of being able to talk freely without feeling like I was on the verge of having an anxiety attack. For the duration of the night into the early morning, we danced, talked, drank, and ate wings and fries. He introduced me to his homeboy, Totta--the same guy that Jonzella was dancing with. When the fellas left for the bar, I had to thank Jonzella for suggesting that we go out. For the life of me, I was trying to figure out why the dude's nickname was Totta.

Then, it dawned on me; his nickname had something to do with guns.

"See, talking to the man isn't that bad after all, now is it?" she spat before giggling and drinking the rest of her Patron shot.

"Not at all. I hope our brothers don't come over here and embarrass our asses."

"Girl, those fools are gone with two big-boned women."

"Good," I replied.

Soon as we finished chatting, the fellas came back with another round of drinks and food. With a blank facial expression, one would've never known that I was extremely happy on the inside. I knew without a doubt that this night was one of the best nights I've had in a long time—thanks to the handsomely, dark-skinned man that occupied my mind daily.

Chapter 3

Dank

Saturday, December 3rd

Three things I didn't play about were my family, money, and self. After discovering what Baymatch was doing to my cousin, I had all types of fucked up thoughts in my head. I wanted to do some foul shit to his family; however, Totta told me to leave those thoughts alone. That God would handle him accordingly.

I was really hoping that going to the club last night was going to help me stop thinking about Colt. It did, but briefly—while I was chopping it up with Ms. Lady, aka Jonsey, at Club Freeze. From the time I saw her walk into the club, she had my mind on quiet mode. When I saw her staring at me as if I had her hypnotized, I knew I had to say something to her. Not one time did I regret approaching her; she had a beautiful personality—the little that she showed me. Jonsey's vibe was phenomenal, even for me. As we talked and danced, I wished that I would've pressed the issue of us hanging out months ago.

Caught Up in a D-Boy's Illest Love

We've seen each other around town before and held pleasant conversations. Normally she would clam up and pull away, but last night she wasn't on the shy tip. I was thankful for that since I needed her to help me forget the type of day I had earlier. At times, I couldn't fully enjoy our conversation, but looking at that fat pussy between her legs put my mental in its rightful place. At the closing of the club, we exchanged numbers.

Soon as Totta and I left the club's parking lot, the foolery of Baymatch and Colt was back on my mind. At five o'clock in the morning, when I stepped through my front door, I pressed my cousin to tell me every detail of what took place between him and that rapist. Once Colt gave me the rundown on every sick thing that Baymatch had done to him and ordered Colt to do, I found myself face down, ass up in front of my toilet.

The images of what Colt described were sickening. Seeing him distraught and feeling as if he was less than a man was even more sickening. Knowing that all those times I saw him happy, he really wasn't. He was miserable, depressed, and felt as if he was alone. Not being there for my cousin made me angry with myself. I was always raised on being there for my family, yet I failed to be there for Colt. From five o'clock until I woke up at noon, that shit drove me mad. Totta came back over my house around 12:15, pouring shots of Patron.

"Woe, have you talked to Colt since he left this morning?" Totta's deep voiced shouted from the kitchen's bar.

My heart began to race as I thought of all types of things that could've happened to him. Sitting erect on my sofa, I said, "Nawl, what's wrong?"

"They saying he going crazy in Bibbs Circle," Totta quickly said as he rushed out of the kitchen with no glasses in his hands.

"Why?" I inquired as I looked at Totta with a worried look on my face.

"Dunno. It's so much he say, she say shit that I can't get a clear understanding," he voiced as he stood in front of me.

Not wanting to sit still anymore with a pounding heartbeat, I hopped off the sofa and rushed to the china cabinet that housed two of my tonka toys: a twelve-gauge shotgun and a semi-auto shotgun. One thing I knew was that I had to be strapped going out to Bibbs Circle; it was like baby Iraq out there. Those niggas didn't give a fuck about a shootout.

Caught Up in a D-Boy's Illest Love

With my weapons in my hand, I grabbed my keys off the key holder, locked, and closed my front door. Running towards Totta's silver Yukon truck, I was ready for the bullshit, and so was my partner. Starting the engine, Totta peeled away from my crib.

"Any word on Baymatch?" I inquired as he hit the gas pedal.

"Nothing other than he was shot twice. His folks got a two thousand dollar reward out for any information."

Nodding my head, I kept quiet. I was wondering who was going to come out of hiding and say that they saw me pull up at his house earlier. I knew someone saw me or Colt slide through that man's front door; hopefully, folks kept their damn mouths shut.

Getting back to the task at hand, I asked, "Who fucking with Colt?"

We were eight minutes away from Bibbs Circle, the most hood projects in Montgomery. Normally, I would be praying that we made it out of baby Iraq safely; however, today I wasn't in the praying mood.

"Mark...Yam Yam's baby daddy."

Looking at Totta's blackened, long oval-shaped face, I burst out laughing. I laughed until I had tears in my face.

"Are you fucking serious?"

"Yep," he replied as he jumped on I-85 South.

"Mane, I brought the heavy shit over Mark's dumb ass?"

"Yep, because you know where we going. You know them niggas dumb as fuck out there."

"Today is not the day we finna die over some bullshit," I announced to myself more so than to Totta.

"Roger that."

There was no need in me asking Totta what part of Bibbs Circle was the chaos taking place. I already knew the heart of the project land was our destination. Soon as we pulled onto Dartman Drive, we saw crowds of dusty, black to well put together individuals gossiping amongst themselves.

Before my partner put his truck in park, I hopped out, but not before saying, "Let's get this shit over with."

"Ain't naan gon' fuck with Colt!" my cousin yelled angrily.

After hearing him, Totta and I ran to the scene. It didn't take us long to reach my cousin, whom was being held by two dudes that were taller but skinnier than him.

"What's up, Totta and Dank?" a group of females cooed as we fled past them.

Caught Up in a D-Boy's Illest Love

Ignoring the broads as we approached a shaking, pissed off Colt, my voice boomed with, "Let him go!"

"I can't do that, Dank. It's too many kids out here," the guy behind Colt expressed calmly.

"Woe, let him go. Ain't nothing gonna happen with these kids and elderly folks out here," Totta voiced sternly.

On the other hand, I wasn't quite sure. Colt was already a mess from yesterday's incident. So, I was very sure that he didn't give a damn about kids or the elderly being present.

In a split second, 'ah shit' and 'somebody gonna say something' rippled through the crowd, followed by a strong, cocky male voice saying, "That two-thousand-dollar reward gonna have somebody talking. Whoever killed Baymatch, the streets gonna tell it."

The dudes who were holding Colt let him go as they walked off in search of the latest news.

"Colt, let's go," I voiced as I scanned every face near us.

Slowly turning his head to me, Colt began to walk. Totta and I weren't far behind him as we looked into some of Bibb Circle's residences faces. I was ready to get the fuck away from the most ratchet projects in the city. My breathing wasn't normal until I was sitting comfortably in the passenger seat. Shortly after, Totta peeled away as I began asking Colt questions.

"Colt, what the hell happened?"

"Mark kicked in Yam Yam's air conditioner while her and I was fucking. Soon as the nigga saw me, he pulled his gun out and pulled the trigger. The gun jammed up on him, giving me time to bust that nigga in the face with a floral vase," my cousin stated emotionlessly.

"You know that nigga act crazy about that girl, so why you even fucking with her?" Totta inquired as he made a left turn onto Fairview.

"It ain't like they are together," that twenty-four-year-old nigga spat aggressively.

Before turning around to look at him, I shook my head at his dumb remark and angrily said, "That pussy gonna get you killed."

Shrugging his shoulders, he slumped down in the seat at the same time he looked out of the window with an angry, ugly, long face.

Ring. Ring. Ring.

Facing the front, I pulled my cell phone off the holster. Jonsey's name was flashing across the screen.

With a blank facial expression on my rounded face, I answered the phone with a smooth, "Hello."

"Hi. Did I catch you at a bad time?" she asked as Totta's phone rang.

"Nawl, Ms. Lady, you good," I replied as my partner said, "What's up, sexy?"

"Umm, I really don't know what to say but the truth so...I called so that I could hear your voice," she voiced sweetly in that innocent, proper tone of hers.

That once blank facial expression now had turned into a smile.

"Is that so?"

"Yes," she replied happily. I could tell by the way she responded that she was smiling.

"Are you busy tonight?"

"Sort of," she replied with a heavy sigh.

"Make time for me. Call me back with a time, Ms. Lady."

"Will do."

After saying niceties, the call was ended. Immediately, I knew that Jonsey was my target. I aimed for her because she was gullible, easy, and seemed like she didn't ask any questions. I couldn't lie like I didn't want her something bad, because I did. Everything about her made me want to punish her for clouding my judgment whenever I saw her.

Caught Up in a D-Boy's Illest Love

Upon putting my phone into the holster, I noticed that we weren't going to my home, and that Totta was grinning with the phone up to his left ear.

Not giving a damn about him being on a call, I rudely asked, "Nigga, where are we going?"

Ignoring me, he piped in the phone, "Aye, sexy, I'll be pulling up in two minutes. Are you standing by your car?"

Well, I guess I got my damn answer. I hope he ain't on no quickie type of mission, I thought as I had to endure the fake, sweet talk he was making, followed by him saying, "A'ight."

"Colt, you okay?" I asked as I looked at him.

"Yeah," he replied, but I knew that he was lying.

"Dank, you asked me where we going?" Totta asked as he threw his phone into the semi-clean console.

"Yep."

"Finna pull up at a broad's job…City Gear. Time for me to wine and dine her ass while getting her hooked, and then…oops, cut that ass off," he laughed while turning into the packed, yet small, shopping mall.

A lie wasn't shit for a nigga to tell. Little did my partner know, I saw him and lil' shawty before. Now was the time to bust his ass on that fake lie he tried to sell me.

"Nigga, you been fucking around with ole girl you seeing now and ole girl from last night," I said as I pointed at the petite, dark-skinned female, standing in front of an older model silver Camry.

"And your point?" he asked seriously, pulling beside ole girl's whip.

"Shid, you feeling one or both of them, mane. You would've been cut things off. It's been three weeks, and I know you don' got some ass already. So, stop trying to play that role with me, nigga. Them broads got you wrapped around their fingers," I laughed as he opened the door.

"I do shit for a reason, my nigga."

"Hmm, hmm. Nigga, you better stop doing that. Bitches will kill you about their feelings," I replied before he closed the door.

Quickly opening the door, Totta spat in a matter-of-fact timbre, "That statement coming from a nigga that only fucks a female twice and never calls them back again. Put them on block and act as if he don't know them in public...tuh!"

"Bye, dude," I chuckled as I waved my hands for Totta to exit his vehicle.

With Totta macking ole girl and the radio on low, my mind was all over the place. I tried to think of Jonsey naked, but that didn't work. Placing my focus on Colt was hard as hell. I took my eyes off him and tried to kick off a conversation. That shit failed miserably once I saw his lonely, lost facial expression.

God knew I wanted to be there for him, but I honestly didn't know how. I remembered my grandmother telling me that if someone was in distress that talking could help them. So, I politely begged my cousin to speak to me.

"Colt, talk to me please."

"There's nothing to say."

"Tell me how are you feeling."

"Like I'm useless, a piece of shit, a punk, a good for nothing type of nigga...that the world would be a better place without me."

"Colt, you can't feel that way. Soon as we leave here, we gotta drink and talk. You crashing at my crib, and that's an order."

"A'ight."

Caught Up in a D-Boy's Illest Love

As we waited for Totta to finish macking ole girl, I decided to not pressure Colt anymore. I needed some entertainment; thus, me texting Ms. Lady.

Me: *You squeezed me in your busy schedule yet, Ms. Lady?*

I knew females were quick to text a ninja back, so I had my eyes glued to the phone as I awaited her response. Hell, I didn't get that damn response until an hour later—as I was laid up on my cozy, white sofa.

Jonsey: *Sorry, I'm replying so late. Um, how does 7 sound?*

Wanting to be petty and not respond 'til an hour later, I chose not to.

Me: *That's cool. Your house or mine?*

Jonsey: *Um, neither. How about food and drinks? Texas Roadhouse?*

Not the one to be seen in public with a broad that wasn't going to last long, I sighed heavily as I pondered her question. Truth be told, all I wanted to do was fuck so that I could get my mind off my cousin and Baymatch. I didn't want to fuck Trasheeda since her sex game didn't help me the other night.

Jonsey: *???*

Me: *Yeah, that's cool.*

Caught Up in a D-Boy's Illest Love

Jonsey: :)

What the fuck is that shit she just sent me, I thought as I stared at the two dots and slash. Shaking my head at the remark, I yelled, "Aye, Colt, you gon' be alright by yourself for a little while tonight?"

"Yeah," he replied from the kitchen.

"Where are you going, nigga?" Totta stated while smacking on a tuna sandwich.

"To fuck after I wine and dine lil' mama from the club."

Ms. Lady would be the perfect catch to do whatever I wanted done—if need be. It was nothing for me to make a female do what I wanted, when I wanted. All I had to do was drop a stack or two of money at them, and they fall for whatever I say. Their panties slide off, easily; their thoughts and morals disappear, quickly, and there I am like a thief in the night taking their whole damn soul.

I'm finna catch your ass slipping, Ms. Lady, I thought at the same time Totta looked at me and said, "I highly doubt that. She's a tough cookie. Damn broad almost a virgin…according to her sister."

"They all are almost like virgins before I peel them panties off," I chuckled.

"Mane, I bet that you can't fuck her tonight?"

Caught Up in a D-Boy's Illest Love

"Bet, my nigga," I yelped happily as I started pulling money out of my front pocket, and then I quickly continued. "What's the amount, my nigga?"

"A stack."

"A stack it is," I said as I counted out ten, crisp hundred-dollar bills.

Leaning over to shake his hand, I had a wicked smile on my face as I knew that I was going to be one thousand dollars richer.

"You know I win all bets. Get ready to run me my money when I get back, boy!" I boasted as I ran upstairs to get dressed.

"You fucking with a grown woman ... not no little girl," he joked.

"I learned all of my slick moves from the best two women in the world—Geraldine and Gloria...don't forget that nigga. That pussy gonna be hooked on me, and that's the end of discussion. I'm finna own Jonsey!"

***

Strolling into Texas Roadhouse with Ms. Lady on my arms had a nigga breaking out in hives. Never has there been a time when I went out in public with a broad that I wasn't in a relationship with; that was an ultimate no-

no. However, desperate times called for desperate measures. I was dying to know what Ms. Lady screamed and felt like.

"Table for two," Jonsey's soft voice stated to the thin hostess while she smoothed her red scarf around her slender neck.

Later on tonight that same scarf going to be around your legs while they are up in the air as I am beating up your lovely guts, I thought as I eyed her.

Within seconds, we were being seated in front of the packed bar. Getting into the role of the charming smooth talker that I am, I began to lay it on thick.

"You look absolutely gorgeous, Ms. Lady," I voiced as I licked my lips all the while eyeing her.

"Thank you." She blushed as the crowd at the bar hoot and hollered as the game displayed on two big screen TVs.

Surfing through the menu, Jonsey's hands were shaking, and I knew she was nervous; thus, me making polite comments to ease her mind. Our alcoholic drinks were delivered, along with the hot buttered rolls. Neither one of us knew exactly what we wanted, so we sent the waitress on her way. Halfway through her drink, she began to loosen up; thus, signaling to our waitress that she was ready to place her order.

Go ahead and loosen up a little bit more for me, Ms. Lady. We need some sex after this, I thought as I gulped down a triple shot of Patron.

"What would you like to have, ma'am?" the thick woman stated, happily.

"Chef's salad with no onion and extra ranch dressing, and another Kenny's Cooler, with an extra shot of Patron."

"Okay, and you sir?" the woman asked as she planted her big, brown eyes on me.

"T-Bone steak well done. My sides are seasoned rice pilaf and green beans, and I'll have another triple shot of Patron as well."

After repeating our order, the thick chick waltzed off. With my eyes roaming over Jonsey, my dick immediately reached its peak. Engaging us in a light conversation, Jonsey held my attention without thinking about sex, which was the first for me. Realizing that she was getting to me, I turned the tables.

"Are you a virgin?"

Chuckling, she replied, "What kind of asshole question is that?"

"Just a question."

"No, I'm not. Does that hurt your feelings?" she asked before cocking her head to the right.

"Nawl. Just didn't want to ruin your life with my expertise."

Laughing while putting the pink straw to her mouth, she replied, "How do you figure I'm not going to ruin your life?"

"And there is the tipsy, non-shy, Ms. Lady," I laughed.

Our dinner was served and the drinks kept coming; well, for me that was. I had to cut Jonsey off from drinking since she drove her car to the restaurant. Our conversations never ceased. They grew more interesting once I let my mind get off bedding the chick and winning the bet that Totta and I had in place.

Damn, she's a pretty cool chick. Very interesting, I thought as she told me what she wanted out of life, which was to own an outreach program for African American youth.

"Dank, my ninja!" I heard one of Totta's cousins, Jap, say excitedly as he strolled towards the table with three gorgeous broads around him.

"What's up?" I said as we dapped each other up and the ladies spoke to Jonsey.

"Coolin'."

"It's been a long time since I've seen you out and about...dating and shit," he chuckled.

"Go sit yo' ass down somewhere," I said in a joking manner, but I was dead serious. The last thing I needed was for Jap to say the wrong thing out of his mouth.

Chuckling, he bent down and in a low tone he stated in my ear, "So, this is the broad that you and Totta got a thousand-dollar bet on?"

"Yep."

Nodding his head, he stood up straight at the same time wet shit splashed on my face and on Jap's green shirt.

"Well, shit. I'mma holla at cha later, Dank," Jap stated quickly as he extended out his hand.

After dapping him up, Jap and his ladies disappeared from the scene. Looking at Jonsey, I was shell-shocked at her behavior.

"What's wrong with you, woman?"

"You are truly a piece of shit!" Jonsey stated in a matter-of-fact timbre as she began to throw everything on the table at me.

"Broad, what the fuck is wrong with you?" I asked as I hopped up and glared into her big, glossy eyes.

"A thousand-dollar bet," she hurtfully spat before standing up.

Laughing her comment away, I said, "What are you talking about a thousand-dollar bet, Jonsey? The alcohol got you tripping."

"I can read lips just fine. Tipsy or not, I can recall the entire conversation between you and that mini pimp," she said as she flagged the waitress down.

"Then rehash it, Ms. Lady," I egged on.

"So, this is the broad that you and Totta got a thousand-dollar bet on?" she stated before continuing, "Tell your little pimp friend the next time he wants some shit to be between the two of you...that he should make sure that is mouth is not visible. I'm sure I'm not the only one that can read lips."

Trying to think of something slick to say, the only thing I could come up with was, "That's not what he said."

"Fuck off, Casey," she voiced before walking off.

Seeing that there was no way out of the lie, I sat there and waited for the waitress to come back with the receipt as I watched Ms. Lady exit the building. The inner voice in my head informed me to run behind her and apologize, but the dog in me said fuck it. If I was meant to sleep with her, I would.

Caught Up in a D-Boy's Illest Love

Within three minutes of seeing Jonsey's car speed away from the restaurant, I felt like an asshole. Things were going great between us, and my mind wasn't solely on bedding the interesting woman. I was actually looking forward to chatting more with her. She was the first female, outside of my grandmother and mother that could put my mind at ease.

Huffing and puffing at my failed mission, I stated to no one in particular, "Nih, ain't this 'bout a whole bitch! Damn you, Jap."

Chapter 4
Jonsey

Monday, December 5th

Lunch was calling my name. I knew that I didn't want chicken or a hamburger. Thus, I decided that it would be best for me to grab a sub sandwich from the hood store on Highland Avenue. I was glad to be off Walmart's clock, even if it was for an hour. Customers worked my nerves about the latest electronics that they had to have in their homes for their spoiled rotten children. Christmas was twenty days away, and I would be glad when it was over with.

Zooming across the parking lot to enter the chaotic noon lunch traffic on Ann Street, I almost hit two boys who were taking their precious time crossing the street. Completely pissed off, I blasted my horn and yelled, "Get the fuck out of my way!" I knew they couldn't hear me since my windows were rolled up. Yet, I felt relieved yelling at the little bastards.

The south's weather was totally crazy. One minute it was hot and the next it was cold. Out of all the days, today was the day it was in the low fifties. I had the heat control set on hell—that's just how cold my body was. I couldn't take temperatures below seventy degrees very well—unless I was snuggled underneath piles of my covers.

Pulling into my favorite hood store in Montgomery, it was beyond packed with people. My eyes fell on the one person that I was avoiding running into—Casey. I was completely disgusted at the sight or thought of him since the failed dinner at Texas Roadhouse.

Even though he disgusted me, he was still a sight for sore eyes. Knowing that he was a grade A asshole, Casey was handsome as he wore a red-collared shirt, black pants, red Timberland boots, and a black and red skull cap. Gold jewelry was wrapped around his neck and right wrist. Before I knew it, my brown peepers were ogling the handsome dark chocolate, five-six, broad shoulders, and lean built man.

Quickly realizing that he was a waste of my time, I parked my car by the non-working gas pumps, shut off the engine, and stepped out of the car. The wind blew hard and I ran inside of the busy store. Soon as I stepped inside, the medium-sized store was filled with conversations and laughter. Not wanting anything but a sandwich, I made my way towards the sandwich/salad station.

"Excuse me," I casually stated several times as I walked in front of patrons at the checkout counter.

Finally arriving at my destination, I stepped to the back of the line only to be greeted with a bright, gold smile from asshole himself as he held two two-liter Sprite drinks and three bags of honey roasted peanuts.

Why can't he be a normal man? Why does he have to be an asshole who likes to make bets about bedding a woman? I thought my mood turning sour.

"Ms. Lady, how you doing?" Casey's deep voice spoke calmly.

Silence.

There was no need in him asking me shit!

"Oh, so now we don't speak to each other?" he continued.

Silence.

"I'm sorry for Friday. That was very immature of me. I hope you accept my apology."

"Hmm, hmm," I replied as I slowly strolled up the shortening line.

"May we start over?"

Turning around to look him in the eyes, I nastily spoke, "Not a cold day in hell will we ever start over again."

"Are you sure?" he probed as he stood closer behind me.

"I don't associate myself with assholes. I been left those days alone. I'm sure there are a lot of thirsty, moral-less women throwing themselves at you. Ones who wouldn't mind you making a bet to fuck them."

I didn't realize that my voice carried until some of the patrons of the store said, "Well, got damn it, now."

Nodding his head with a smile on his perfectly crafted face, Casey replied, "By the middle of next year, you'll come around to me. Anyways, have a Merry Christmas."

Not responding to his comment, I watched him walk away as he answered his phone while handing his homeboy the items he had in his hand. Before he walked out of the door, Casey looked at me and nodded his head. Instantly, I had a scowl on my face.

"Who the fuck does he think he is?" I mumbled before placing my order.

Twenty minutes later, I was sitting in my car in Walmart's parking lot eating and thinking about Casey. At one point, everything about him had me seeking more. I loved his swag—casual clothing wearer and hood, yet well-educated. The way he talked from time to time changed; one minute, he used slang, and the next, he was talking as if he was a college professor. True enough, in the past I did clam up whenever he talked to me longer than two minutes, but please believe that I was listening to him converse with others.

Looking in my rearview mirror, I placed my eyes on myself and said several times, "He's not the one, Jonsey. One day you will find the right man for you. Casey isn't the one! So, please stop letting him invade your brain."

Ring. Ring. Ring.

Retrieving my phone from the console, I saw my sister's number display across the screen.

Sliding my hand across the answer button, I said casually, "Hello."

"Hey. How's work?"

"Exhausting. These people are working my last nerve. How's your day?"

"Work is cool. Going by slow as hell though. Renee keeps calling my phone talking about she's sorry and that she wants to come and visit me," she replied as I heard her shuffling through some papers. Jonzella worked at a physician's office as a receptionist.

"Wow. She's still trying, huh?"

Caught Up in a D-Boy's Illest Love

"Yep, and honestly, it's kind of annoying. I don't understand why she's trying to be in my life all of a sudden. When I sent her that message on Facebook, it was to let her know that I forgave her. I don't want anything to do with her," Jonzella replied in a low voice.

"Are you sure that you forgave her?"

"Yep."

"Have dinner with her."

"Bitch, I wish I would have dinner with a motherfucker that didn't make sure that I had dinner when I was a child. Fuck her. I have a family, and she surely isn't that family."

"I'm sorry she ruined your day. Let's change the subject."

"Are you going by the house before you go to class?" Jonzella asked in a blank tone.

"I wasn't planning on it. Why?" I inquired as I exited my car.

"I forgot to grab my Calculus book."

"Typical you...always forgetting something. Ugh! I will have time to go home and grab it," I responded honestly as I hit the lock button on my key fob.

"Thanks a bunch. Oh, I didn't forget to take out a pack of pork chops and that bagged corn for dinner," she laughed.

"No, your greedy ass isn't going to forget to take out dinner. Bye, cow, I must hit the clock. Love you. See you at school."

"Love you more," she sweetly replied before hanging up the phone.

Strolling into Walmart with slumped shoulders, I thought about my best friend turned sister. Jonzella Marie Brown was originally named Jonzella Marie Johnson. Every evening Jonzella was at my home, eating dinner, getting disciplined, being loved and nurtured by my parents, myself, and three siblings, and sleeping. After a week of the same repeated behavior—no supervision and no food—from Jonzella's mother, Renee Johnson, my parents decided that it was best to adopt a seven-year-old, Jonzella. My brothers and I surely didn't mind because we loved Jonzella just as much as she loved us. Honestly, it was a godsend that I finally had a sister instead of my knucklehead brothers.

"This store stinks," an elderly woman replied from behind me as a male and woman chuckled.

Caught Up in a D-Boy's Illest Love

Slightly turning around to see the people behind me, I huffed upon seeing Casey and two older looking, but pretty, women.

"Momma, don't start no mess in these folk's stores. You say that every time you come in here," the younger of the two older women happily stated.

"I don't know why I chose to drive y'all to the store. Momma, you could've driven. You know Grandma bad in any store she frequents," Casey voiced before lightly snickering.

Zooming away faster from him, I was glad when I reached the break area. I had four minutes until it was time for me to clock in; therefore, I used that time to scroll through my email account. I was desperately looking for another job. One that was less stressful and fit my persona—a desk job.

Three minutes of surfing my account, I shoved my phone into the back of my pants and began walking towards the electronics department. Halfway to my destination, I ran into Casey.

Not looking his way, he laughed and said, "How was your lunch?"

The hairs on my neck stood, a tingling sensation formed all over my body, and the inappropriate thoughts formed. Not wanting to address him, my crazy self did anyways.

"Great," I replied quickly before becoming a sarcastic butt. "Now, you have a great day."

I hoped he got the hint of my voice and behavior. I was sure he did when he responded with a, "That's what's up, Ms. Lady. I'll let you get to work. Don't want to get you fired or anything."

The entire time he talked his eyes were locked into mine. Shivering, I sped past him without a care in the world.

"Casey, who's that gorgeous doll you were talking to?" I heard from behind me.

Eager to hear his response, I slowed down as he answered, "A unique little woman."

"Well, you should get to know her. I sense good vibes from her other than that last little tramp you were dating."

There's no way in hell you will get to know me. Y'all have created an asshole, and I want no parts, I thought soon as I stepped foot in the electronics department, which was filled with angry shoppers.

Clearing my head and throat, I announced loudly, "Who's the next person that needs help?"

Caught Up in a D-Boy's Illest Love

***

I was in La-La Land as Professor Johnston was talking about some shit I wasn't interested in. Doodling on a piece of paper, my thoughts were on Casey's response of "a unique little woman".

I had to know what he meant by his response, granted that he made a bet about me. Knowing that I had been involved in a prior incident of a bet, for whatever reason, I couldn't stop my thoughts of Casey. I wondered how cozy his arms would be wrapped around me. I asked myself did he snore when he was asleep, what his likes and dislikes were, if he knew how to cook, and if he knew how to use that dick that was down his mid-thigh. At the thought of his man part, I became aroused at the thought of him having amazing sex— something I hadn't had in over a year; well, with a real-life dick that is.

"Ms. Brown, can you tell me what economic equilibrium is?" my economics teacher voiced loudly, interrupting my thoughts.

"Huh, oh, um, the economic equilibrium is when the supply equals the demand of a product while the equilibrium price exists somewhere in the 'supposed to be' supply and demand curves intersect," I quickly responded as I lifted my head.

"Very well then, Ms. Brown. So, you were listening," my sassy-mouthed professor stated before walking her thick self towards the right side of the small-sized, plain Jane classroom.

"How in the hell can you understand this stuff?" a classmate in front of me whispered.

"Hell, I don't know. I was surprised that I got it right. This chapter is completely harsh to interpret. I just Google it and try to get a better understanding in easier terms," I whispered back.

Twenty-five minutes later, Professor Johnston's class was leaving her classroom with a thick study review packet for the finals, which was seven days away. I really wasn't pressed to start my week with studying, which always led me over studying on the weekends. Economics was my worst class; I had to study extra hard to maintain a B+. Psychology and Algebra were a piece of cake, so there were no complaints. Ready for the late afternoon to be over with, I scurried along to my next class—Psychology.

"Jonsey!" I heard my sister scream as I strolled out the door.

Caught Up in a D-Boy's Illest Love

"Stop screaming my name like that, Jonzella. I hear you," I casually voiced as I waltzed towards her.

"Sorry. There was a lot of chatter around me. So, I wanted to make sure that you heard me," she replied as we were in close proximity.

"Hmm, hmm," I stated while pulling my book bag in front of me.

Unzipping my bag, we lightly chatted about our weekend. Upon her retrieving her Calculus book, Damion Greene and Jackson Pierce spoke to us.

Sighing heavily, I gave a weak hello as Jonzella sang, "Hellloo, fellas."

Damion and Jackson have been trying to date my sister and I since we arrived at Alabama State University (ASU), three years ago. Damion was seeking Jonzella's company, while Jackson was seeking mine. He wasn't my type, and I grew tired of telling him that. They were fine brothers, don't get me wrong. I just wasn't going to waste my time with a guy that stayed in a lot of females' faces. I'm selfish, and I don't like to share—men that is.

Annoyed at the fact that Jackson was trying to talk to me, I simply stated, "I don't want to be late for my next class. Sis, I'll see you at home. Love you."

"Love you, more."

Strolling off, Jackson was on my heels.

Sighing underneath my breath, he spoke, "Jonsey, why won't you give me a chance? I'm not a bad guy."

"I'm not interested in dating right now. Work and school are my priorities right now."

"They are mine as well, but I would like to get to know you," he said genuinely as he strolled along with me.

"For the two-hundredth time, no Jackson."

"I'm nothing like Sebastian Mox," he voiced in a jealous tone.

Slap.

"Don't you ever speak that fucking name around me again! Matter of fact, stay the hell away from me!" I yelped after I slapped Jackson's face.

People around us came to a halt as I angrily stared into Jackson's face. Tears were beginning to form, but I forbade them to drop. Thinking on something positive caused them to go away as I turned on my heels. I had a class to get to.

"I...I didn't mean any harm. I just—," he yelled as I continued walking away.

The fucking nerve of him to bring that useless male name up, I thought as I ran to my next course.

Caught Up in a D-Boy's Illest Love

Upon entering the cool classroom, I became paranoid. I wouldn't look anyone in the face. When they spoke, I gave them a dry hello. The mentioning of the cruelest guy at ASU always put me in a bad place.

Sebastian Mox was the most gorgeous guy on campus. To my surprise, he asked me out. Eagerly, I accepted—not knowing that there was a bet in place for how quickly he could bed, dump, and then humiliate me. A three hundred damn dollar bet was established between the football jock and his buddies.

Thank God, I lucked up and found out about the bet by running into his buddies, whom were talking amongst themselves on the side of a dorm building while smoking weed. I was one pissed, hurt female. My little world was shattered as I realized that I was being made a fool of. The sweet nothings, nice acts were all part of Sebastian's game to get me naked while slandering my name. That established a no-dating zone for me.

Why are you giving Sebastian such a hard time but not Casey? A thought formed in my head as I took a seat at my normal table and chair.

One is no better than the other. One had a higher bet to bed you than the other. Both are males, and both are extremely handsome. So, why does Sebastian get a harsher punishment than Casey?

As the questions continued, I couldn't find one solid damn answer. All I knew was that I was pissed. When I analyzed each question, I noticed that I was more pissed at Sebastian because I really liked him and believed everything that he said. I guessed I wasn't expecting for him to make me feel as if I was just another piece of ass to him.

My thoughts were interrupted soon as Professor Norman closed the brown door and announced in a sloth-like manner, "Today, you guys and gals will be working on your study guide for the finals next week. Retrieve your books and pencils, this guide will help you effectively prepare for the test."

Everyone in the classroom sighed as I smiled and finally exhaled while thinking, *good, my mind needs to be somewhere else.*

Chapter 5
Dank

No matter when I saw Ms. Lady, she always captivated my mind. Her big, bubbly eyes and shy persona turned me on—easy prey. Ms. Lady wasn't swole in the ass and thighs department, but she had a little some some I could grab on. Within the last three years that I've grown accustomed to seeing her, each time I wanted to carry our conversation further—the bedroom type of further. Giving that I was in a relationship, I refrained from doing so. A nigga was fresh out of the tainted relationship, and I was ready to mislead and drive someone's daughter crazy.

Relationships and I weren't good, so I wasn't pressed on being in one anytime soon. I had to live the bachelor's life for a while until the right one crossed my path.

Ring. Ring. Ring.

Glancing to the right to look at the cracked screen on my phone, I shook my head as I said, "Why is this buzzard calling me?"

Caught Up in a D-Boy's Illest Love

Not removing my gloved hands to answer the unwanted call, I continued bagging the large quantity of Ice. I had several callers that were seeking the potent dope, and I was ready to serve the Iceheads.

My phone stopped ringing only to start back. Growing annoyed at the caller, I slid off the black glove and aggressively answered the phone.

"What, guh?"

"Why are you answering the phone like that?" my ex asked.

"Diamond Crosby, what in the fuck do you want? I knew I was very clear that I didn't want any parts of you."

"Dank, I'm sure that we can work through this rough patch of our relationship. We have never had an argument before, so why are you letting this thing blow out of proportion?" her soothing voice stated curiously.

Sighing heavily, I sternly replied, "It was a mistake that we had gotten together anyways. You and I would have never crossed paths if I hadn't gone to physical therapy for my shoulder. You were in my life for a season. That season is over with, so please leave me alone."

As she continued on about why we were meant to be, I rehashed the day I met her. It was in the summer; the first day of physical therapy for an injury that I received playing ball with Totta, Colt, and two buff niggas from The Savage Clique named Baked and J-Money. Diamond was my assigned therapist. Her looks surely didn't pull me to her; it was her attitude—positive and outgoing. Twenty days of therapy, it was bound for the two of us to get to know each other. She asked questions, and so did I. One thing led to another, and we were in a relationship.

"Dank," she softly said that brought me into reality.

"Look Diamond, I appreciate you for being a great therapist and all, but you are one sucky ass girlfriend. You did the one thing I can't tolerate. You are too friendly with these niggas in the streets. I don't want a friendly ass woman."

"I could say the same for you."

"Well, there you have it. You see we ain't good for each other. I wish you well; now please stop calling me."

"I love you, Casey," she huffed.

Laughing, I said, "Nawl, you love my money."

"I make just as much money as you."

"Nope, your paychecks in two weeks don't equal the amount of money I make in three days. It was nice doing this...whatever. I'mma see you around," I replied before hanging the phone up in her face.

For the next fifteen minutes, Diamond continued to call my phone. Realizing that I wasn't going to answer the phone, that heifer loaded my phone full of texts, which I didn't read. Immediately, I trashed all of them.

Ding. Dong.

"I know damn well this bitch did not pop up at my crib," I mumbled as I didn't move a muscle.

Ding. Dong.

"I know this nigga in here," Totta voiced as he began beating on the door.

"Nigga, if you don't get away from my door with that foolishness!" I yelled as I left the unsacked crystal-like dope on the glass, circular table, aiming to let my homie inside.

Soon as I opened the door, we dapped each other up. Upon him closing the door, he said, "Where's Colt?"

"Have no idea. I haven't seen or talked to him since I left Saturday night."

"Have you called Ms. Donna?" Colt's mother was the last person that I had wanted to call, but I had no choice but to given, that I was worried about my cousin.

"Yeah, she said that she hadn't seen him either."

Caught Up in a D-Boy's Illest Love

"Do you think he might be—" his thick voice stated before being cut off by our ringing cell phones.

"Yo," Totta spat in his phone as I strolled to answer mine.

Picking up my phone, I quickly answered it as my front door opened, followed by Totta stepping across the threshold.

"Wait...repeat that one more time," I said into the phone as I swore I misunderstood what my mother was telling me.

"Colt's dead. From what the police told Donna, he shot himself in the head," my mother's sad voice stated.

"When did he do it? Where was he at?"

"Today at Oak Park. Not sure of the time, but Donna just called me two minutes before I called you."

"Damn, man," I sighed as I shook my head, praying that I was dreaming.

Immediately, my head dropped as low as it could go as tears formed in my eyes. I knew I shouldn't have left him in the house by himself Saturday; I should've been there for him. There was no way, I should've been entertaining the idea of fucking anyone's daughter when my cousin was desperately in need of someone to be there for him. I didn't know what to say as I apologized to Colt repeatedly in my head for leaving him to deal with the bullshit that was revealed from Baymatch's mouth some days ago.

I'm so sorry, Colt. Damn it, man, why did you have to leave? I had your back, I thought as my mother said, "Casey, are you okay?"

"No, Ma, I'm really not. Colt was going through something that I can't tell you, and I should've been there for him more so than I was," I told her as I tried not to break down.

My front door opened, and it was hard for me to hold my head up. When I did, the look on Totta's face told me that I had to get off the phone.

"Ma, I'll be by sometime today."

"Okay, baby. I love you," she replied in her motherly tone.

"I love you more."

Placing the phone in my lap, Totta said, "What's wrong?"

"It's apparent we didn't get the same news, so you spill your news first."

"Two niggas broke into our spot and stole the work. Danzo got them niggas and two others at his crib tied up. What's your news?"

Caught Up in a D-Boy's Illest Love

"Colt killed himself."

"Woe, I know you lying," he voiced as he sauntered towards me with his head and shoulders low.

"We deal with the dope first, followed by dealing with the mourning over Colt," I stated as I quickly bagged the remaining crystal meth.

***

"Once my partner pulled the duct tape off one of you niggas, y'all better be telling us where is the rest of our fuckin' dope?" I voiced sternly to four light-skinned, scary looking niggas as they squirmed in the brown, hard bottom chairs.

All we saw were the niggas moving their heads as they murmured. Totta snatched a small piece of tape away from one of the dudes mouths; his victim had a small afro on his head.

"Speak," Totta informed the skinny dude.

"My brother and I don't know anything about dope, other than what Danzo inquired about. ToTo and Benut called our name as they were standing in front of a house with three Walmart bags," the guy quickly stammered.

"Who's your brother?" I inquired, squinting my eyes at the dude.

More murmuring came from the fourth dude as he moved his head from left to right.

"I'm assuming this dude here is your brother?" I asked him as I pointed to the fourth dude.

"Yes," skinny guy answered.

"Danzo, which two niggas did you see with bags in their hands?" I asked the six-foot one trapper of the Westside.

Pointing at the first and second dudes in the chairs, Danzo's silky voice said, "Them lil' fuck boys. They are known for breaking in folk's cars and homes. Some niggas on the Northside just whooped their asses four days ago for trying to break into their shit."

Peeling the tape away from the first two guys mouths, I glared at the idiots. Not in the mood for lies and unwanted conversation, I looked at the two accused thieves and asked, "Where's the rest of the dope?"

Neither of them said a word. They just glared at me. Seeing that they weren't going to answer, Totta walked over to the stereo. Seconds later, the volume on the stereo increased; followed by the first guy jumping as if hot coals landed on him.

Caught Up in a D-Boy's Illest Love

Totta shot his dumb ass, I thought as blood began to ooze out of buddy's left knee. Volume decreased before Totta snarled, "One more chance. Answer my partner's question."

The third and fourth guys began moving their heads and squirming in the chair, which prompted me to snatch the thick, gray tape away from their lips.

"Speak," I commanded nastily.

"We don't know anything about what's going on. Can my brother and I leave?"

"Danzo, who are these two niggas?" I asked the old trapper.

"Some niggas that cop weed and Molly's from me. They are regular Joes though, but I still snatched they asses up...just to make sure they weren't in on the stealing," he voiced as he tugged on the knot on the back of his black durag.

"Do you think they were?" Totta questioned, never taking his eyes off none of the guys.

"Nawl," Danzo replied as he looked between Totta and me.

Looking at the first two guys, I had a question of my own that would allow the decision to be made on whether or not to let the third and fourth niggas leave.

"These two niggas y'all boys?"

They replied, "Yeah."

But the second dude offered, "But they didn't take anything. They were strolling down the street when we saw them."

Nodding my head, I told Totta to cut them loose. I couldn't lie like I didn't admire the second dude's courage and honor for standing up for the third and fourth guys; most niggas weren't going to clear anyone's name but their own if they were caught in a jam.

"So, where's my shit?" I asked the remaining assholes for the final time.

"We only took the six Ziploc bags filled with dope. Two Ziplocs per Walmart bag," the first guy offered, quickly.

"What's your name first one?" Totta asked.

"Jamarcus, but folks call me Benut."

Totta asked the second dude his name, and his reply was, "Ronald, but my nickname is ToTo."

Nodding his head and looking at me, Totta increased the volume as I fired a bullet into the first dude's, Benut, left shoulder.

The volume resumed low as the third and fourth niggas bolted towards the front door before Danzo told the freed guys, "Keep your mouth shut about your friends, who finna receive a grand ass whooping."

"We will," they responded while nodding their heads. Once they were out of the door, Danzo ensured that it was closed and locked.

For the next three minutes, Totta and I drilled the guys. They kept saying they only took three bags, but I knew that was a lie. Tired of the questioning, I placed a bullet in the second guy's, ToTo, head as Totta put two in the Benut's cerebellum.

"Clean up time," my partner and Danzo said in unison while they put on their gloves.

"How many bags are left?" Totta asked curiously.

"Ten."

With an 'oh shit' facial expression, I sighed, "Totta, what?"

"They had taken six bags, right?"

"Yeah," I replied in an agitated tone. I prayed like hell we just didn't kill two niggas for no reason.

Say it ain't so, I thought as I stared at Totta.

"Shit, Dank. I forgot to tell you that I sold four bags earlier this morning."

All Danzo could do was laugh and say 'oh shit' repeatedly, while I stared at Totta like he had lost his mind. My anger rose as I briefly glanced at the dead bodies on the dirty, suede brown sofa.

It took me a moment to get my thoughts together before I angrily told Totta, "We gotta finish this shit!"

Three hours after the senseless murders, clean up session, compensating Danzo for us using his trap house to conduct business, and discarding the bodies, I was ready to grill out my partner for the minor slip up of not informing me about sales. However, I wasn't completely in the mood to deal with him at the moment—given that Colt invaded my mind.

One minute I felt that I wanted to go on a killing spree and the next, I was laughing and smiling at the stupid things my cousin would say. Out of all my male cousins, Colt and I were the closest. As I pulled onto my grandmother's street, Totta's cell phone rang.

"What's up, sexy lady? Speak to me." That seemed like it was the new hey for him.

Several seconds later, he was informing me that he was going in to speak to my family before disappearing to Alabama State University (ASU), an HBCU. Quickly glancing at him before we dapped each other up, I nodded my head and said, "This new chick got you wining and dining her ass, huh?"

Caught Up in a D-Boy's Illest Love

With a smirk on his face, he replied before closing the door, "I'll be back in thirty minutes, woe."

Sighing as I glanced at my grandmother's teal door, I shook my head. I wasn't ready to waltz in since I knew Colt's mother was inside, crying up a storm.

"Dang, Colt, why did you do this man?" I inquired, hoping to find some type of clarity.

My nerves got the best of me; thus, me facing the mourning. Soon as I strolled inside, Cousin Donna broke out in tears.

"I can't believe my baby is gone," her husky voice cried out.

"Me either. We were just hanging out Friday," I announced as I shook my head in disbelief.

Within ten minutes, my grandmother's home was flooded with family members. Overwhelmed by crying and sad faces, I retreated outside. At least outside in the cold, I would be able to escape.

"What's up, Dank?" one of my younger, trying to be a dope girl, cousins spat.

"Shit," I responded as I wanted to give her a life lesson about the streets.

"You heard the latest news of Baymatch?"

"That he's dead?"

"Nope."

"Then what?"

"Folks speculating that one of his male lovers might've killed him."

With a blank facial expression as I stared into my boyish looking cousin, I said, "Well damn," while thinking, *well, they are right...in a way*.

Having enough of family time, I told her, "Aye, tell my momma and grandma that I'm gone home. Anyone else pulls up looking for me, tell them that you haven't seen me since earlier today."

Nodding her head, I closed the door and put the gearshift in drive. It was one quiet, lonely ride to my crib as I thought about Colt and all that he endured from being a needy, fatherless child to trying to be a dope boy to actually being a do boy to being molested by Baymatch.

In need of something to drink, I decided it was in my best interest to pull up at a liquor store. Never amazed at how packed the place could be, I quickly shut off the engine and hopped out. Soon as folks saw me, they were giving out their condolence. After two minutes of saying, "thank you," I was ready to get home and out of sight of people. Probing questions from two people pushed me over the edge.

"Stop asking me shit that I can't answer. If you want to know why he did it...shoot yourself in the head and ask him."

Gasps were delivered from several people's mouths as I stepped further into the line. Those same pestering fuckers found the exit door quickly. I drifted off into a small world of my own. A light, familiar voice said, "I would like two Smirnoff peach bottles, please."

Not in the mood to flirt or work her nerves, I simply let Ms. Lady be.

"What can I get for you, Dank?" the slim cashier of a woman stated with a sympathetic look upon her face.

"A box of Newport shorts, two original packs of Swisher Sweets, and two bottles of Patron," I replied, pulling money out of my right pocket.

A light tap graced my left shoulder. I slowly turned around and stared the big-eyed beauty in her face.

"Sorry to bother you...just wanted to say I'm sorry for your loss."

"Thank you," I replied as I thought of who told her that I lost my cousin.

Caught Up in a D-Boy's Illest Love

The cashier brought my items, rung it up, and I handed her the money. Grabbing the big black bag, I began to walk towards the exit door.

"Casey, if you want to talk...I'm just a call away."

"I'll remember that."

"Talk only," she lightly chuckled.

Bringing a smile to my face, I turned to face her before saying, "I most definitely will remember that."

Chapter 6
Jonsey

Wednesday, December 7th

My classes were cancelled today, and I was alright with that; especially after the day I had at work; I wasn't in the mood to deal with walking, carrying books, or sitting in three hard chairs. Soon as I clocked out, I was relieved. For the next three days, I was off, and Walmart was going to be the furthest thing from my mind. It would be buried deep inside of my economics book, hopefully. My mind was heavily on Casey's feelings, but I didn't call or text him. I prayed heavily that he found peace and that he was alright.

Two days ago, when I saw him at the liquor store, he was closed off from the world; the sight of seeing him in such pain made me feel so sorry for him. I didn't know his cousin personally, but I've seen them two around town together; I saw the love amongst them. Colt and Casey were very close, so I knew the pain he was feeling was very deep.

Ding. Ding.

Caught Up in a D-Boy's Illest Love

Sitting in Indiana-style on my made bed, I reached for my cell phone. Immediately, butterflies crept into my stomach as my hands began to tremble while a huge grin was on my face. Within seconds, the happy emotions were replaced with caution, given that this could be another one of his tricks to bed me. Some guys were sick in the mind. Who was to say that he wasn't going to use his cousin's death to try and peel my panties off—all the while pretending to be a gentleman.

Staring at the phone, I said to myself, "He did have a bet out on how fast he could sex you. Keep that in mind before you go falling head over heels for this dude, Jonsey. Just be a listening ear...nothing less, nothing more."

Casey: What's up, Ms. Lady? Is the invitation for texting and calling still available?

Me: Yes, it is.

Casey: Is it cool if we talk on the phone?

Me: Sure.

Casey: A'ight. I'm finna call you.

There was no need in me responding to the text because his name was displaying across my phone's cleaned screen. On the third ring, I answered the phone.

Caught Up in a D-Boy's Illest Love

"Hello," I smiled as I flopped on my bed and glared at my ceiling.

"It took you long enough to answer the phone," he laughed.

Chuckling, I replied, "No, it didn't. I answered the phone on the third ring. So, tell me, how you are doing, Ms. Lady?"

"I'm doing well, and yourself?" I asked, blushing.

"Great now that I am talking to you."

Still blushing with a huge grin on my face, I replied with, "Is that so, sir?"

At the same time I thought, *Nih, bitch, you know you could've said something other than that. He just said he was doing great since he was talking to you. That was your cue to go in for the kill,* my inner voice stated as I became nervous. What my little mind should've been doing was on the cautious side, but instead, it was all open for anything that Casey said.

"That is very much so. All my folks want to talk about is funeral arrangements, pallbearers, singers for Colt's going home celebration, and other sad shit that I'm tired of hearing. Since, my cousin passed I'm constantly hearing talks of burying him. So, I decided that I should hit you up just to escape from the hells."

"Understandable. Well, I guess I can let you use me in a non-sexual way to escape what you are dealing with," I replied honestly.

"Well, dang, you don't have to put it that way," he snickered lightly.

"What other way should I say it, sir?"

"Not in those words...it seemed so harsh," he quickly replied before continuing. "Jonsey, I need to properly apologize for what you overheard. I was wrong for even doing such a dehumanizing thing like that."

Feeling happy, but still on the cautious side, I responded, "I forgive you, Casey."

"I really appreciate it, Ms. Lady. Woman, I gotta ask you this...you must be shy or som'?"

"A little."

"You gotta break outta that, Ms. Lady, especially if we are going to be hanging around each other."

I was baffled at the mention of him saying if we were going to be hanging around each other.

"Been this way all of my life. Granted, if we are on cordial status I'll break out of it. I'm like this around people I don't know...very well," I confessed as I placed my left leg over my right.

Caught Up in a D-Boy's Illest Love

"Maybe one day…hopefully, soon, you will be able to carry on a conversation with me without shying up on me," he breathed silkily.

"I'm not clamming up on you now, am I?" I questioned in a matter-of-fact timbre.

"No, because I'm not in your face," he laughed.

"Oohh, low blow, my friend. Low blow," I snickered.

We chatted on the phone for over an hour. No topic was safe; well, sexual comments weren't safe. I enjoyed our conversation, and I was sad that it had to end due to my cell phone being on five percent.

"You have a good day, Ms. Lady."

"You as well."

Chuckling, he spat, "When I see you face to face, I want you to be as carefree as you were on the phone with me."

Laughing, I replied, "I surely will…try."

"You gon' miss your blessings being shy, Ms. Lady. Now, charge up your phone, and call me soon as it gets on one-hundred percent," he announced.

Smiling, I happily responded, "See, you already being bossy. I'll call you once I'm on one-hundred percent, sir."

"A'ight," he replied before we ended the call.

Caught Up in a D-Boy's Illest Love

Hopping off the bed, I happily slammed my charger into my phone. Whistling and skipping to my desk, I retrieved my economics book, study guide, notebook, and a pen and pencil. As I took a seat, I heard Jonzella walk through the door.

"Jonsey!" she playfully yelled.

"Yes, deary."

"I decided to ditch school today as well. Thought we could study together and watch a movie afterwards," she replied as she sauntered down the hallway.

"That's fine with me. I'm just now getting into my economics study guide," I sighed with a smile on my face; apparently my mind decided to imagine a smiling face Casey as we talked on the phone earlier.

Stepping into my room, Jonzella strolled towards my work study and gave me a hug. Immediately, she had to start with the questions.

"You must've seen Eleven Golds...I'm sorry...Casey, today? What was said? Are y'all going to redo that botched dinner date? Is he coming over? Are you going over to his house? How's he doing with the death of his cousin? Bitch, tell me something," Jonzella's high-pitched voice inquired quickly while her arms were still draped around me.

Caught Up in a D-Boy's Illest Love

"No, I didn't see him, but we talked on the phone for an hour or so. We just chit-chatted...nothing personal. He apologized. No to the dinner date, him coming over here, or me going to his place. He's doing as well as can be expected given his cousin is no longer breathing. He's tired of the mourning talk," I replied as I glared at the right side of her face.

"Well, at least y'all are making some type of progress. Next time y'all talk, suggest the redo of a dinner."

"I'll pass on that. As of now, I'm just going to be an ear for him to vent. Nothing less, nothing more. Sorry, Jonzella, but I'm going on the cautious path," I responded, hoping that was the truth.

"Understandable, but don't fuck around and be too cautious. You'll miss the chance of being with him. I'm sure you don't want the next unworthy bitch to have him. Then your tail will be looking crazy."

"That ship between Casey and I has sailed off to Neverland," I told myself more so than her.

"Yeah, right. If it had sailed off...you would've never told him to call or text you if he needed someone to talk to."

Quickly defending myself on my intentions of being a shoulder for him to lean on, I spat, "Look...so I had a mild crush on him for three years. The bet destroyed any hope of trying to get to know him better. So, Jonzella, please chill with that. Within three weeks, Casey and I will no longer be conversing on the phone. My choice!"

Standing in front of my face, Jonzella replied, "Now, that's a damn lie, but okay. Anyways, I'm hopping in the shower before I bring my study items."

"Okay."

Two hours of studying went by fine, until our mother called my phone. She had so many questions ranging from what Jonzella and I were doing, to whom Kevin and Kenny hung out with and when was the last time we saw or spoke to them, and finally, to when would we be leaving out for Christmas and heading to Myrtle Beach, South Carolina.

Her constant rambling didn't bother me until I saw a puzzled look on Jonzella's face, when our mother mentioned Kevin and Kenny's name, for the second time; however, this time it sounded as if she was extremely worried about them.

I opened my mouth to inquire about them, but Jonzella spoke first, "Mom, what have those two bird brains gotten into?"

Caught Up in a D-Boy's Illest Love

Our mother's reply was simple and curt, "Nothing that you ladies' father and I can't handle. You know they are always doing something to be the ones to get all of the attention," she nervously replied with a fake chuckle.

"You should've sent them to a boot camp or something," I stated as I shook my head and wondered why they had to cause so much trouble. It wasn't like our parents neglected any of us.

"Anywho, you ladies get back to studying. Father and I love you. Oh, don't forget to call your older brother...he's starting to think you ladies don't love him," she fussed.

"I called him today, but he was at work," Jonzella said.

"I'll call him as soon as we are done studying," I replied before sticking my tongue out at Jonzella.

"Splendid," our mother stated before we ended the call.

"What in the hell has Kevin and Kenny gotten themselves into now?" Jonzella asked.

"Heck if I know. Those two always doing something, and I really don't understand why. They have so much to offer, yet they don't want to do anything with their lives. Well, I'm not going to worry over them like I've been doing. I got a future of my own I'm trying to build."

Caught Up in a D-Boy's Illest Love

"Well, I'm finna call and grill their asses out! Momma didn't sound normal when she kept inquiring about them, so I gotta see what in the hell they did," Jonzella voiced as she smacked her left thigh.

"Go head then Detective Brown. Close my door on your way out."

Hopping off my bed, she dialed one of our brother's numbers.

Closing the door, she replied, "What the hell?"

Not entertaining her question, I tried to focus on my study guide; fifteen seconds of trying to focus, I grabbed my cell phone and dialed Casey's number.

On the fourth ring, he answered his phone, "Hey, Ms. Lady. How was studying?"

"It was goo—," I was cut off by Jonzella's loud voice saying, before she bursted into my room.

"Those niggas phones off. Whatever they did...it had to be bad. Oops, my bed you on the phone."

Shaking my head with a stern look on my face, I pointed towards the door, signaling for her to get out, as I said to Casey, "I'm sorry about that...sibling drama. Now, what set of interesting topics are we going to explore?"

"How about a movie and dinner?"

Caught Up in a D-Boy's Illest Love

"Not going to happen," I replied sternly.

"Please...pretty please with a cherry on top. I'll be on my best behavior. I need to get out of this house," he whined, sounding like a wounded dog.

Bursting out in laughter, I replied, "If you promise to never try to whine again in your life."

"Deal," he laughed and then continued. "Meet me at Longhorn's in thirty minutes."

"Okay," I replied.

Hanging up the phone, I quickly cleaned my study area and dressed—all the while with Jonzella in my face, smiling and asking questions. Fifteen minutes later, I was skipping out of the home and talking to myself.

"Stay cautious. Don't do shit you don't have any business doing, Jonsey. Keep it strictly friendly...not that ogling type of friendly."

Chapter 7
Dank

I had to pressure little mama to get out of the house; I was going insane staring at nothing but knuckleheaded, hard legs. I love my partner Totta to death, but he and Danzo were working my fucking nerves with the talks of Colt and the funeral arrangements. The news of ToTo and Benut's bodies being found traveled fast, which led those niggas to my crib. Neither of us was sweating when we learned of it; we had a thorough plan put together. If those two niggas that we let go snitched, then we had something for their asses as well.

"Y'all make sure y'all don't break under pressure. I'm sticking to my line. I'm a third-time offender. A bitch gonna have to come with it to give me my AIS number again," Totta huffed while pulling on his fat blunt.

"I second that, homie," Danzo replied as he snorted a line of coke.

Shaking my head at him, I wondered what possessed him to snort that shit. Not in the mood to ask him, I stated, "Tomorrow, we will rehearse this shit, but not at my house. I'm tired of looking at y'all. I'm finna head out to eat and to the movies."

"Yo' ass trying to make up for the fuck up…oh wait…where is my stack of money, nigga?" Totta laughed.

Going in my pockets, I pulled out ten crisped Benjamins. Handing the money to him, I said, "A bet is a bet, and I lost."

"Like I knew you would…thanks to Jap doing what I asked of him."

"Wow," was all that I could say before shaking my head.

"I'm tired of losing bets, woe. You be taking my funds and shit," he chuckled as he ironed his pink collared shirt.

"I been learned to stop betting with Dank. Nigga, got a smooth two thousand from me," Danzo replied as he wiped his nose.

"Y'all niggas have a great evening…as I will," I told them as I closed and locked the door behind me.

Seeing them hopping into their whips, I was sitting in my front seat repeating my rehearsed lines. There was no way I was willing to have an AIS number assigned to me. Even though we did fuck up and murdered those boys, if their asses hadn't stolen in the first place, they would be still living—I guess.

From the time I left my crib to arriving at Longhorn's, I was completely absorbed into what I had to say if the homicide detectives rolled up at my spot. Soon as I stepped out of the car and placed my eyes on Jonsey, my thoughts of the detectives ceased only to be replaced with, *damn, she is one sexy, beautiful individual.*

With a wide grin upon her face, Jonsey sexily waved at me. Strolling towards me in a pair of black jeans, a tight fitting pink shirt, and black booties, her little body swayed as she stated, "Hello, friend."

Friend, I thought as I spoke, "Hello, friend. I hope you are hungry because I surely am."

"Come on. I have already spoken with a hostess. Our table should be ready."

"Look at you taking charge and shit," I replied as I went in for a hug.

The scent of sweetness quickly ran into my nostrils, and I inhaled the tantalizing scent deeply. The feel of her body was just right against mine. Her skin was soft, her grasp against my waist was tight, which resulted in me not wanting to let her go. Several light taps to my back informed me that she no longer wanted to be held.

Wrapping my hand around hers, we ambled inside of the busy establishment. Several patrons were enjoying delicious meals and drinks which they accompanied with light chatter and laughter. Seated in the far back in a booth, I took in the young beauty. I noticed that she was nervous, and I didn't want her to be. I had to find a way to make sure that she was never nervous around me again.

"I see you are clamming up on me again," I stated as I flipped the menu, even though my eyes were on her big, brown peepers.

"Some like that," she giggled.

"Why?"

Exhaling heavily, she stated, "I probably shouldn't be telling you this, but I've had a mild crush on you for three years. Since the first time I placed my eyes on you. So, you tend to make me nervous."

Intrigued by her having a crush on me, a nigga showed his eleven golds and pearly whites. I didn't see myself as a handsome nigga. I wasn't ugly, but I never been the type to be obsessed with the way I looked.

"Are you blushing?"

Caught Up in a D-Boy's Illest Love

"I am," I beamed as a thin waitress came to our table.

After we ordered appetizers and drinks, we resumed conversing. I noticed that she couldn't keep eye contact, her voice shook, and her hand trembled.

Lightly chuckling as I moved from in front of her to sitting beside her, I voiced, "Now, what kind of shit is that? You can look at me when we first speak and when we part, but in between us conversing you turn away."

"You make me nervous," she cooed.

"What about me that makes you nervous?" I inquired as I glared into her perfectly rounded face.

She said umm several times before responding with, "You are so confident of yourself. It's the look in your eyes. The way you carry yourself. Then things go back to how I feel about myself. Do you see a young woman or a little girl? Am I good enough to be in your company, minus the bet that you made?"

Nodding my head after she finished talking, I had to figure out the best way to respond. I knew I couldn't dismiss the last thing that she said, but I wasn't going to dwell on it first.

"I hate that I make you nervous. I really don't know what to say other than to be yourself around me. As far as what I see, I see that you are a hardworking woman and student. You are far from friendly. The main question you should be asking is, am I good enough to be in your company? You should never doubt yourself. You know who you are better than anyone in this world, so why doubt yourself?"

"I'm one of those people that aren't street smart like my sister and brothers. I'm the reserved, quiet type. I mind my business and keep it moving. I believe there are good qualities in everyone, which caused me a lot of headache growing up."

"Stick with me, and you will have all the street sense that you need. Now, there are good qualities in everybody; however, everybody may not want to show you their good qualities because they feel you are unworthy of seeing it. Understand what I mean?"

"No."

Chuckling, I replied, "For instance, my partner, Totta. In my eyes and eyes of a few, we see him as a damn good person. The unfortunate will see him as a stern asshole who only gives a fuck about his money. The reason he's like that is because he knows that there are some people in the world that don't want him to do good and want to see him struggling and in a fucked-up place."

"Ahh," she replied oddly. I knew then that she really didn't understand, so I had to break it down for her.

"Totta is the type of person that will give you his shirt off his back and deplete his bank account for you. Totta is loyal to those that are loyal to him. He's really a soft bear when it comes down to those that he loves and cares about. I'm the same way. If I fucks with you, I do. If I don't, you will know. My actions are going to show it. Jonsey, there's a certain attitude that you must have dealing with the streets. You have to know that there are good people that do bad shit for no reason at all," I stated before taking a sip of my drink, and then I continued. "You can't be nice to everyone because that's a quick way to get your feelings hurt. People will use you for their benefit. They will play underneath you just to get what they want."

"Understandable."

"Do you really understand, what I'm saying?" I asked curiously as I touched her hand.

"I do. My folks used to tell me that all the time. When does Totta show people that aren't kin to him that he has good in him?"

"Every month. He volunteers at the Boys and Girls Club on the weekends. During the holidays, he buys gifts for all of the children and has a Christmas party at the main center."

"What good do you have in yourself?"

Smiling, I shook my head and refused to answer the question.

"Oh, no, you are going to answer the question, sir," she giggled.

"You gotta become my girlfriend to figure that one out."

She began to pout, and it was the cutest thing that I saw. I couldn't tell her my good thing that I did. Hell, Totta nor my family knew.

As Jonsey was about to press me again, I felt a cold hand on my shoulder followed by a raspy voice saying, "My dear, Casey. It's a pleasure to see you before Sunday."

Turning around to stare Mrs. Wilson in the face, a smile appeared as I got up to give her hug. She introduced me to her son and his wife. We spoke, and of course, I knew that Mrs. Wilson was going to hold me hostage for a few moments.

"Hi, Mrs. Wilson. How are you today?" I asked.

"I'm fine. There is no need in me asking how are you because I see that you are doing just fine with your beautiful date," she sweetly responded to me before she said hello to Jonsey.

Jonsey nervously waved hello, which prompted Mrs. Wilson to say, "What book are you reading me this Sunday?"

"Oh, this is the gentleman that comes by the home and reads to you, Mother?" her stocky son inquired with a twinkle in his eyes.

"He surely is, Waymon," she replied not looking at her son.

"That is so sweet of you, Casey," Waymon's wife cooed.

Quickly glancing and nodding my head at the wife, I saw the look in her eyes that she wanted to fuck. Stifling laughter back, I stated to Mrs. Wilson, "I thought you promised that you weren't going to tell anyone our secret."

"Oops, you know an old lady forgets. Apologies," she lied with a smile on her face.

"Well, since you are being nosey and can't wait for Sunday. I have a nice selection for you. I have a Sci-Fi book, a chivalry romance novel, a World War II love story, and *The Little Woman* book."

"Why isn't there a mention of an erotica book?" she asked with a raised eyebrow.

Caught Up in a D-Boy's Illest Love

I shook my head as her son groaned and the ladies said ooou. My response was, "Mrs. Wilson, I'm not going to be responsible for you getting pregnant. I will buy you any erotica book you want, but I shall not read it to you."

"Mama, you shouldn't be reading books of that nature," her nerdy son voiced in an annoyed tone.

"How do you think you got here? It surely wasn't from a big ass white bird. Your father and I did some nasty things to get you in my womb."

My head dropped as I laughed. Mrs. Wilson was a straight to the point, no beating around the bush type of woman. I loved her spunky attitude, her views of the world and people, and how she was determined to not lose an ounce of respect or love for a son that sent her to a home upon getting married. The same son that lived in the same city as his mother and came to visit once a month—on a third Wednesday. There was no way in hell I would be seeing the woman that birthed and cared for me once a month, let alone in a retirement home.

"Anywho, Casey, you do have a nice selection. I'll let you choose the book since I know that you will make a great choice. Well, I've taken up quite a bit of your time.

Caught Up in a D-Boy's Illest Love

I will see you Sunday at..." she left the sentence lingering for me to answer.

"I will be there at nine a.m."

Eyes bright with a huge grin on her face, she replied, "Oh, someone is staying until supper time?"

"I am. I pulled some strings to have y'all a nice dinner prepared for the holidays by my grandmother, mother, best friend, and self."

"You know I'm trying to stay fit for Mr. Johnson to see my curves, now," she chuckled before her son said, "Ma, please stop it."

The laughter erupted from Jonsey, Waymon's wife, and a couple of patrons of Longhorn's. After Mrs. Wilson and I hugged again, we said goodbye.

Taking a seat next to Jonsey, she sweetly voiced, "So, you reading to Mrs. Wilson is your good deed?"

"That and so much more," I replied as I smiled in her face.

***

Dinner and a movie was a success. Not one time did I have any inappropriate thoughts of bedding Jonsey. After the movies, I decided that I wasn't ready to end our night. The visitation of parks was closed due to it being night time, so I settled on us going down to the riverfront to continue our conversation.

The wind was howling as she snuggled into her dark gray jacket. With the hood over her head, I could barely see her small, rounded head.

"We can sit in the car if it's too cold out here," I voiced as walked into the tunnel.

"No, its fine...for now," she stated through clenched teeth.

"Are you sure, Jonsey?" I inquired, pulling her close to me.

"Absolutely."

"Since we have left Longhorn's, you've learned quite a bit about me. Now, it's your turn to tell me a little bit about you."

"I'm attending Alabama State University for a Bachelor's Degree in Business. I'm the fourth of five children. As you know, I'm somewhat shy. Been an employee of Walmart for two years, as you probably already know. Umm, I love to color, read, and listen to music. Oh, and sing when no one is around. I hate cats and dogs. I cannot swim."

"Wait, you cannot swim?" I laughed.

"Not at all."

"Well, damn. I guess I gotta teach you then."

"I guess so," she replied as we took a seat on a lone bench.

"Jonsey, why aren't you in a relationship? You seem like a good woman whose head is in the right direction, no drama, and no games."

"It seems that relationships and I aren't meant for each other right now. Every time I think I'm interested in someone, I find out that they are not who they claim to be or they make ridiculous be...umm, simply put, I'm not ready."

Awkwardly, I glanced at her. I wanted to ask her a question, but I didn't want to put her in a sour mood. Before I got the chance to change the subject, her soft timbre said, "You have something to ask me?"

"I do, but it's not worthy of being said."

"Go ahead. I'm a big girl."

"What I did to you was wrong, and I truly apologize for that. Has that ever happened to you before?"

"Yes, my freshman year at ASU."

"Did you really like that guy?"

"Yep."

Feeling like the true asshole that I was, I tried to find some comforting words. However, Jonsey was true to her words—she was a big girl. She laughed that particular conversation off, and the remainder of our conversation went in a breeze—until my lips graced hers. For a moment, I thought she was going to get up and run away; but instead, she pulled me closer to her, followed by diving her hot, wet, slender, long tongue into my mouth. Without a moment's hesitation, Jonsey was sitting in my lap as I hungrily sucked on her lips and tongue.

The wind was whistling and blowing as steam quickly enveloped us. Hands began to roam the non-private parts as we explored the depths of our mouths. Her kisses were enough to turn a drunken man sober. She was one of those passionate kissers. I knew that I should've pulled away, but I couldn't. Her body felt so right in my arms; yet, I had to pull away or she would've ended up in my bed. I didn't want that—yet.

"I think we are getting carried away," I said into the howling wind.

Nodding her head, she opened her mouth to say something, but nothing came out. As I noticed she was struggling to speak, the longing in her eyes confirmed that she wanted my lips against hers, again.

Caught Up in a D-Boy's Illest Love

For a few moments, we glared at each other before she finally spat, "I think I should be going."

Not wanting to part ways from her, I simply replied, "Okay."

As walked hand in hand, there was an eerie silence between us. I wondered what she was thinking, but I dared not to ask her. My mind was on how cool and amazing she was which informed me that I had to spend less time with her. I didn't know where my heart lied, and I surely didn't want to ruin her thoughts of how she viewed love and happiness.

"You have a good night, Casey," she announced as she approached the hood of her car.

"You as well," I voiced as I turned her around for a hug.

Nodding her head before pulling away from me, Jonsey disappeared inside of her car, started the engine, and tooted the horn before she drove away. As I stood in the cold, I wondered what in the hell I was going to do next. Going home to sulk in misery was not an option; thus, me pulling out my cell phone to make a call.

"Hello," the sultry voiced freak spoke.

"You at home?"

"I sure am," Trasheeda spoke eagerly.

"I'm on the way over."

Caught Up in a D-Boy's Illest Love

"Hmm, just the type of dick I need in my life."

Hanging up the phone, I hopped in my car and peeled to the one person that could make me nut in five minutes. In my eyes, she was the best head giver I've ever had. It had been that way since we were in junior high school. Trasheeda was the standby pussy; she finally came to terms with her position with me. She was not to be employed full-time with the dick. Trasheeda was fine being the seasonal help.

Soon as I pulled into her driveway, my cell phone began to ring. Seeing Jonsey's name on the screen, I quickly answered the phone.

"Hello."

"I just wanted to tell you that I enjoyed your company tonight."

"I enjoyed yours as well."

"Well," she began to say before I cut her off.

"Are you busy? Are you going to sleep right now?"

"No."

"Do you want to talk to me on the phone?"

"I do...if you want to."

With a huge smile on my face and my right hand on the gear shift, I placed it in reverse at the same time I responded, "Of course, I do."

Caught Up in a D-Boy's Illest Love

Maybe Trasheeda was not the route for tonight, I thought as I sped down her street, heading to my home all the while talking to Jonsey.

Chapter 8
Jonsey

Wednesday, December 28th

After our makeup date, I noticed that Casey wanted to be around me more. I assumed, with it being closer to his cousin's funeral, he wanted to alleviate some of the pain, which I gladly accepted his invites. I didn't see the need to say no or be cautious; I embraced the closeness between us. We decreased the amount of time we were on the phone with each other, and replaced it with spending more time in person. I had to admit that these past three weeks were great between us. As I took his mind off the ordeal of burying a family member, he brightened my mind on topics I would've never thought to engage in.

Four days before Jonzella and I were to leave for Myrtle Beach, I gave him his Christmas gift, which I told him not to open until that day. He was surprised that I had gotten him something as I was overly shocked at him handing me three beautifully wrapped boxes.

"Don't open them until Christmas," his thick timbre added before he planted a kiss on my forehead.

Caught Up in a D-Boy's Illest Love

Christmas was exceptionally wonderful with my family and lovely phone conversations with Casey. Instead of chatting on the phone like we normally did, while I was in a different state, he decided to FaceTime me. He was handsome as he wore the pink, green, and white, button up, Ralph Lauren shirt, that I had gotten him for Christmas. He looked absolutely refreshing in my gift as he wore a pair of crisp, white jeans and boots. A fresh haircut, normal amounts of gold, and a handsome smile greeted and held my attention for the forty-five-minute call.

Towards the late end of Christmas, Casey called me and sadness was in his voice as he tried to pretend that he was alright. It had been two weeks since the burial of Colt. I knew that his cousin was heavily on his mind, which prompted me to soothe his soul and mind.

"Jonsey," Kyvin called out, interrupting my thoughts.

"Yes," I answered as I swallowed the last contents of my hot chocolate.

"Where are you?"

"On the back porch, duh!" I yelled, drawing my feet underneath my butt, all the while observing my parents' beautifully decorated backyard.

Caught Up in a D-Boy's Illest Love

Shortly after, my handsome, medium-brown, engineer of a brother sauntered out the door while shaking his head.

"What's wrong, Ky?"

"I hate to say it but Kenny and Kevin are going to be the death of our parents," he sighed as he sank into a wooden chair across from me.

Exhaling heavily, I replied, "Let's pray not."

"Little sister, that's all I've been doing since they have been getting in trouble with the law."

"What can we do to steer them in the right direction?"

"Hell, if I knew I would've already done it."

Since we arrived at my parents' home, tension had been at an all-time high between my parents, Kenny, and Kevin. I tried to ignore it but the fake laughter, whack conversations, and odd looks amongst them caused me to look at them with questionable eyes. Jonzella finally acted on the odd behavior. Like the inquisitive being that she was, she asked why the tension was so high. Our parents tried to reassure her that everything was fine. Those words went in one ear and out of the other—for everyone at the table.

"What do you think they've done this time?" I asked in a whispered tone.

Caught Up in a D-Boy's Illest Love

"Who knows. Mom and Dad keep saying it's nothing that they can't handle, which lets me know it's pretty bad. They won't even tell me what the hell our brothers had done."

"Same thing she keeps telling Jonzella and me."

With a tired sigh, Kyvin replied, "We will know soon enough. Change of subject."

"Indeed," I responded with a smirk on my face.

It never amazed me how closed lipped our parents were when it came down to Kevin and Kenny; I guess the less they talked about their troublesome boys, the better they will feel about the shit they seemed to get themselves into.

"So, tell me about this guy that has you smiling, and about the guy that has Jonzella glowing."

With bright, brown eyes, Kyvin glared into my eyes as I smiled like a Cheshire cat. The thoughts of how Casey and I turned out were an amazing feeling. True enough, I didn't hope or wish for anything more than what we were; being his friend turned out to have amazing perks.

"He's sweet and dark chocolate, dreamy, dark brown eyes, and a smile that melts my soul. He's twenty-nine years old, no children, extremely smart, and does charity work at a retired home," I smiled as I looked at my older brother.

"What does he do for a living?" Ky asked quickly.

It seemed as if my throat closed up on me as I thought of the answer that I should say. Not wanting to lie to my brother, I surely didn't want to tell him the truth.

"Jonsey, where does this fellow work?"

"Kyvin, why is that relevant?" I asked in a defensive tone.

Taking aback by the timbre of my voice, he nodded his head and replied, "Oh, he one of those types of dudes."

Exhaling sharply, I was not in the mood to deal with the conversation he was heading for.

"Those thugs are not good enough for you. Why must you keep picking those kinds of men to associate yourself with?"

"He is not a thug, Kyvin. If you met him, you would know," I shot back.

"No, thank you. Remember what happened to you the last time you decided to take likes into those particular kinds of people."

Standing to leave, I told my brother that it was nice chatting with him. Before I touched the white door handle, his harsh tone stated, "Don't make me tell our parents what type of man you are involving yourself with. I bet they would have your ass back in South Carolina within a blink of an eye."

Anger soared through me at his threat, "And don't make me tell them that you prefer dick over pussy."

Extremely pissed off at Kyvin, I stormed into the house and ran into Jonzella.

"Whoa. What's wrong with you?" she inquired as she grabbed my hands, which were trembling.

I mouthed, "Ky's bitch ass."

A shocked look was on her face in a second. Ushering me out the front door, she yelled to our parents that we were going for a walk down the street. From the time we left the house until we made it halfway down the street, away from ears, she said, "What happened?"

As I told her the conversation between Ky and me, all she could do was shake her head and say, "Well damn." The topic took a better turn once she asked me how I was really feeling about Casey.

"I like him, but I want to take it slow...given what I've been through with the likes of his kind."

"You know better than anyone what he's really like. However, I think you should continue to take your time with him. At least let him know where you stand with your feelings and all."

"Why should I?"

"Just to see if y'all on the same page."

"Nawl, I think I'm going to leave that alone. If it's meant to be it will happen. I'm not going to force anything on him, especially since he's in a delicate spot with the death of Colt."

"Girl, you gotta be outspoken when it comes to your feelings. Let a nigga know where you stand. Shit, that's what I do...especially after I've been spending so much time with his homeboy, Totta."

"Speaking of that, how long have you and him been kicking it?"

Blushing, she happily replied, "Since the summer. We were just conversing, which turned into sex and more conversations."

With a playful punch to her right arm, I shouted, "So, bitch, when we went out you acted like that was y'all first time meeting."

"We like to role play when we are out in public. It amps things up in the bedroom," she said naughtily as she winked her eye at me.

Caught Up in a D-Boy's Illest Love

Chuckling and shaking my head, she said, "Anywho, you need to be outspoken with Casey. He isn't a mind reader. Just tell him and let things work itself out."

"I've told you too many times that I'm not outspoken like you, Jonzella. I refuse to make an ass out of myself," I whined as I shoved my hands inside of my jacket.

"Ugh, I guess I can help you out a little bit with Mr. Eleven Golds," she sighed with a wicked smile on her face.

"What do you mean help me out?" I inquired curiously as I frowned.

"I'll tell him how you really feel, Jonsey."

"Oh, hell no. Don't do that. That's so high school-ish. Promise me you won't do that," I shrieked as I came to a complete stop and looked at her.

Jonzella planted her big, dark brown eyes on me before saying, "Shit, Jonsey, I hate when you make me promise things. Ugh, I guess I won't say anything to him."

"You gotta do better than that. Promise me."

After several seconds of looking at me, she finally gave in and promised me that she wasn't going to say anything to him.

Caught Up in a D-Boy's Illest Love

Turning around, we talked about school, which was due to start in eight days. I was excited to start back; whereas, Jonzella was not ready to be diving her head back in a new set of books.

Soon as we strolled into our parents' yard, Kyvin was throwing his bags in the backseat of the car he rented as our parents were on his heels wondering why he had to leave so early.

"Stop it, guys, you know I have a busy schedule that I must return to. I want to get ahead of the New Year's work," Ky replied as he shoved the last of his belongings in the car.

You just want to get back to that man you are fucking, I thought as I saw his hands trembling.

"You weren't supposed to be leaving until Saturday, Kyvin. We barely see you in person. Must you really leave early?" my mother whined as she grabbed his left hand.

"Yes, Mother. I must," his agitated voice announced.

Turning on his heels, he sauntered over towards Jonzella and me. Giving her a tight hug and kiss on the left cheek, Kyvin slid a couple of steps to give me a weak hug with no kiss on the cheek. Instead he whispered in my ear, "You won't say shit about my personal life, and I won't say shit about yours. Just don't call crying to me when that thug fucks you over."

Laughing, I replied lowly, "I love you, too, Kyvin. Safe journey."

Inside I was brewing with anger and I wanted to tell my brother's secret, but I wasn't the type to be hurtful. Especially, when I knew that Kyvin had great intentions. I just wasn't in the mood to hear or relive my past.

Chapter 9
Dank

Things around the city were extremely high for Totta, Danzo, and me. Six days ago, Danzo, Totta, and I were scooped by homicide detectives for questioning on the murders of Benut and ToTo. We had our story planned out to the T. Before our story was going to be told, we were going to ask for our lawyers. That was how a lot of niggas got jammed up, talking without the proper representation. There was no way in hell I was going to let those fuck niggas put me behind bars over Benut and ToTo's whack, thieving asses.

Those funky ass detectives kept me in their little stale, cold room for three fucking hours. Sporadically, they came in to ask me, "You sure you don't want to talk?"

Only two words left my mouth, "My lawyer."

The lanky detective nodded his head with a smirk on his face. He had opened his mouth to say something, but nothing came out. The last time the detective stepped into the room, I knew he was going to slap the handcuffs on me. Instead, the punk motherfucker said, "Don't skip town. We'll be back for you and your buddies."

Caught Up in a D-Boy's Illest Love

With a blank look upon my face, I replied, "My lawyer."

"Our plan of killing those snitches today is gone down the drain. What's the move?" Totta questioned as he ceased my thoughts on the interrogation and the promise the lanky, white detective spoke to me.

"Some kind of way, we are going to find those fuck niggas and cease them from living. I ain't finna serve no type of sentence, and I damn sure ain't finna let you or Danzo serve one. No key witness, no case, right?" I voiced as I fired up a Newport while Totta rolled two blunts.

"You damn right. We got their names, and we know exactly what they look like. Now is the time to bring them out of hiding. The main question is how we gonna do that?"

"Do what we do best. Internet those niggas and ask folks have they seen them. The sooner we find them, the quicker this investigation is closed."

"Agreed. I'll start my search now," Totta stated as he placed a blunt to his mouth.

"A'ight."

My phone started ringing. I knew it was money from the number displaying across my screen. Not in the mood to sell anything, I answered the phone anyways.

Caught Up in a D-Boy's Illest Love

"Speak to me."

"You out and about?" the slurred, timbre woman spoke.

"Nawl, I'm posted at my normal spot."

"Okay. I'm on the way to holler at you for a minute," my favorite junkie stated happily.

"Bet."

"Shit!" Totta scolded as he bit his bottom lip.

"What?"

"I can't pull these niggas up for nothing."

"In due time, they will fall in our laps. Just be patient," I spat as my favorite Icehead pulled in front of us.

Ambling towards the passenger side of her car, I hopped in and quickly served what she wanted. Wasting no time getting her away from my grandmother's crib, I hopped out and strolled back to my whip. Totta was on the phone, and by his tone, I knew he was chopping it up with Danzo. Plopping in the passenger seat, I listened to their conversation.

"When was the last time folks saw them girls?" Totta asked.

We didn't know if our phones were tapped or not, so we made sure to talk in code at all times. Girls were code for those two snitches Kevin and Kenny.

"When?" Totta laughed as he balled his fists.

Several seconds later, he replied, "A'ight. I'll just pull up on you."

Hanging up the phone, Totta informed me that the people Kevin and Kenny stayed with said their parents picked them up two weeks ago. They didn't leave an address, and their phones are shut off. With several curse words out of our mouths, all we could do was pray that we saw them soon enough.

After Totta and I smoked blunts in peace, he stated in a frustrated tone, "I need some pussy, woe. Damn, ole girl need to hurry her ass back."

"You got three days, buddy," I laughed.

"That's the fucked-up part about it. I gotta get this pressure off me. Mane, let me make a play. I'mma holla at cha later."

Chuckling, I replied, "You gon' make ole girl nut up on yo' ass."

"I know damn well you ain't gon' tell her...so how she gon' find out?"

"Jealous hoes talk."

"I wish that bitch would. I would slit her throat while my dick in her."

Laughing because I knew he wasn't lying, I shook my head and voiced, "You can't handle pressure to save your life. Don't murder the lil' bih, nih."

"I'll try not to," he laughed while dapping me up.

Watching my homie pull away, I locked my car doors and waltzed into my grandmother's home. She had the kitchen stinking something good.

"Are you okay, baby?" Geraldine, my grandmother, asked sincerely.

"Yes, ma'am," I lied before sighing.

"Casey Eugene Mosley, what you ain't finna do is lie to me. I'm not going to tolerate it," she fussed as she pulled a braided switch from behind the dark brown china cabinet.

Chuckling, I responded, "Grandma, really? So, you gonna switch me today, huh?"

"Hell yes. I know you are in a tough spot right now, and I pray for you, Totta, and the other young fella every night. Y'all will be alright. I know that. Y'all say y'all are innocent, right?"

"Yes, ma'am," I lied again.

Laughing sarcastically, she spat, "Well, sweetie your mother might believe you but I don't. Anyways, do what you have to do to ensure that y'all are on these streets, understood? When this shit blows over...y'all better get out of these streets because they don't love no damn body. Do I make myself clear, Casey?"

"Yes, ma'am."

"You need to get yourself a woman that'll keep your black ass out of trouble. If you had some constant grown woman pussy, then you wouldn't be in this jam in the first place," she fussed as she strolled towards me with the braided weapon in her hand.

"What we are not going to do is have this conversation," I laughed at my grandmother's unfiltered mouth.

"Yes, we are. It's time that you hear it. You running around here with those little skank guppies with all that fakeness running from their head to their toes, got your head messed up and amped to keep up a persona that's not even you. Those hoes don't want nothing but dick and money; get yo' ass a woman that's about having things out of life—a house, a legit company, family, etc.," she sternly stated while I shook my head.

"People hustle to get out of a rough spot not for fame. You had no business then, and you sure as hell don't have any business now doing the shit that you do. We ain't never struggled for shit...not your mother, father, or me. Casey Eugene Mosley, you are an intelligent Black man. You better start thinking about your future. Think about your purpose in life. You are twenty-nine years old…make something of yourself for your future children to be proud of."

Leaning back on the counter, I took heed to what my grandmother had to say. Everything she said was true; however, I had to kill those two key witnesses before I could think about furthering my future. If they didn't die, then my future would consist of having an AIS number and living with a bunch of hard legs.

I chilled with my grandmother for four hours until my mother, Gloria, stepped through the door.

"Hey, Mama," I stated as I got up to hug her.

"Hi, honey. How was your day? What did the lawyer say?"

Sighing heavily, I wasn't ready to tell her what the deal could be. I knew that she was going to cry, and that was something that I didn't want to see. I thought that it was best to get it out of the way.

"If found guilty, the DA is looking at giving us life in prison, which that will never happen because we are not guilty of the allegations they are trying to pin on us."

Caught Up in a D-Boy's Illest Love

Her hands began to tremble as she brought them to her mouth. Shaking her head, my mother cried and I was there to hold her as I reassured her that everything will work out for the best. There was no way in hell she was going to visit me for the rest of my life in someone's institution—nope, not Casey Eugene Moseley!

"Are they going to arrest y'all?" my grandmother questioned as she pressed her thick hands together.

"Don't know. As of now, they don't have any evidence against us other than those two bums that lied on three people before. It looks like we are going to beat this case. From what my lawyer said, the DA don't trust those guys since they have a long rap sheet themselves. On top of lying on previous cases. Their indecisiveness about using their knowledge is highly in play right now."

Eventually, my mother calmed down and glared into my face. The look she gave me scared me shitless because I knew that she was going to ask me that question one more time.

"Casey, baby?" her weak voice stated.

"Ma'am."

"Did y'all kill those boys?"

Caught Up in a D-Boy's Illest Love

"No, ma'am," I lied. My heart was hurting because I lied to the one woman that I've never lied to in my life. I wanted to tell her the truth, but I couldn't. Maybe one day I would, but today wasn't that day.

"Okay. I won't ask you again. I love you, son, and I have your back like I've always had," she softly voiced before placing a kiss on my forehead.

"I love you more. Stop worrying. We didn't do anything wrong. We *will* be just fine." I reassured myself more so than her.

Around eight-thirty p.m., I left my grandmother's home and escaped to my crib. On the way, thoughts of Ms. Lady appeared, and instantly, a sneaky smile was on my face. She finally came out of her shy shell. I enjoyed her company more than she knew. I stopped seeing her as an objective in my unknown game and viewed her as a friend whom I was growing feelings for. In need to hear the chipper, proper voiced young woman, I dialed her number. Like always, it didn't take her long to answer the phone.

"Hello, Mr. Casey."

"Well, hello there, Ms. Jonsey. What you doing?" I asked as I lay back on the arm of my sofa.

"Finally headed back home."

My heart was doing back flips at the mention of her saying that she's heading back to the city.

"How far y'all out?"

"Three hours."

"Cool. May I see you?"

"You surely can," she happily said. I knew she was smiling. Hell, I was too.

"Let me know when you touch back down, and we can meet up."

"Okay."

Soon as I ended the call, Totta was loudly talking at my front door. Before he rang my doorbell, I was unlocking the door. With a huge grin on his face, he was talking on the phone.

"You need to fly home. I need some," he laughed in the phone.

Shaking my head at the fool, I thought, *Shit, shouldn't you be tired from fucking.*

Ten minutes on the phone with Jonsey's sister, he slapped the phone onto the small circular table before saying, "Mane, let me tell you 'bout that hoe, Joanisha. This hoe said I had to pay before I got some of her twat."

Bursting out laughing, he continued talking about the nonsense the freak hoe told him. His facial expressions and what he told me that he told her had me on the floor weak from laughing.

"Woe, chill out. My stomach hurting. So, the entire time you been gone, you was tongue wrestling with a broad about her pussy and mouth?"

"Hell nawl, I took my ass home. Them damn greens Ms. Geraldine cooked had a nigga stomach in knots. Shid, after I used damn near two rolls of tissue, I fucked around and took a whole nap."

Laughing at the fool of a homie, I flipped on the TV. Totta waltzed into the kitchen. He was in need of a drink, and I told him to make me one as well. Sauntering into the living room, he said, "You going over to the ladies' crib with me?"

"Nawl."

"Why not? Ain't it 'bout time you fuck ole girl?"

"Nawl. I'm trying to figure out if it'll be beneficial for me to do so. Lil' mama got feelings for a nigga, and I don't want to fuck her head up."

"Nigga, shut yo' ass up. You falling for her ain't it?" he inquired as he playfully punched my arm.

"Hell nawl. My focus elsewhere. I don't have time for that type of drama right now. I just like chilling with her.

She be taking my mind off shit," I semi-lied before gulping down my drink.

"You know you can't lie to me, right?"

"Ain't nobody lying, dude."

"It's okay if you fell for Jonsey. She's a pretty cool chick. She ain't like that peasant, Diamond, I can tell you that. I can see you and Jonsey settling down and having a batch of churren."

"I'm done with relationships. Once I get my head clear, I'm strictly fucking and minding my own business."

"Boy, shut yo' ass up. In that case, you would've fucked Trasheeda's ass. She been coming on to you pretty hard lately. So, stop lying to me and yourself."

Three hours and fifteen minutes later, our cell phones rung. Before that nigga Totta answered his phone, he said, "My dick finna be super wet! I'mma holla at cha, Mr. Scared to Fuck Som'."

Not responding to him as he ran towards the front door, I answered my phone, "Hello."

"Meet me at IHOP in twenty minutes," Jonsey's silky voiced commanded at the same time my front door closed behind Totta.

"You bet, Captain."

"You so silly."

Caught Up in a D-Boy's Illest Love

"Get off the phone and hurry to your destination."

"Yes, sir," she replied before hanging up the phone.

Dick on hard, I knew I had to alleviate my man before getting around Ms. Lady, or I would be up in her. Before unzipping my pants to beat my dick, I called Jonsey and told her make it forty-five minutes before we met.

Her response tickled me, "Go ahead and play with yourself. Lil' nasty," she giggled before saying okay.

"Mane, I ain't finna play with myself. Bye, guh," I hung up the phone as I began to imagine her naked as I played with her pussy slowly as she rode my dick.

Close to nutting on my hands, I groaned out her name before saying, "I gotta fuck you for real, girl."

Chapter 10
Jonsey

Wednesday, January 4th

Since Jonzella and I arrived back home, she had been staying over Totta's house. That heifer left me at the house by myself; in a way, I was pissed because I wasn't used to being by myself. She told me several times to invite Casey over, but there wasn't a need to do that— given that we were only friends with no sexual benefits. It wasn't that I didn't want to have it with him. It was more so Kyvin's words that rang in my head every time I tried to entertain the thought of asking Casey to come over and the fact that I didn't know how Casey felt about me.

In my mind, it was best that things happened naturally versus me forcing it upon us. There had been several times when Casey could've sparked things off between us, but he didn't, which led me to believe that the timing wasn't right. We had to spend more time together.

Ring. Ring. Ring.

Caught Up in a D-Boy's Illest Love

Grabbing my phone off my pillow, I stared at Casey's name a smile spread across my face. Quickly answering it, I said, "Hello."

"Oh, snaps, you are up early. New classes, classmates, and professors got your nerves rattled?" his deep voiced inquired.

"More than you know," I replied as I rubbed my hands across my face.

"Get dressed. I want to treat you to breakfast before you head off to school."

"Okay."

"Where am I meeting you at?"

"My house. I will text you the address," he smoothly replied.

Not saying a word as my heart rate sped up, all types of thoughts formed in my head.

"Jonsey?"

"Yes?"

"Did you hear me? Is coming to my house too much at this moment?"

Stammering, I replied, "No, no, it's fine. Text me the address, and I'll be there."

"Okay. In thirty minutes, you will arrive at my home, correct?"

Caught Up in a D-Boy's Illest Love

Giggling, I replied, "Aye, aye, Captain."

With the call ended, I sat up in the bed and shook my head. It was 7:30 in the morning, and his ass was up bright and early. I felt a tingling sensation that I felt every morning, and I wished it away. Trying to think of something else, my mind always went to what would happen if I didn't break away from an overly long kiss, how would that hurt our friendship, and what if he had hidden motives.

Eventually, I snapped out of the crazed state I was in and began to get dressed. Twenty-five minutes later, I was sitting in my car as I became nervous of being alone with Casey at his home. Typing in his address into the GPS System, I wished my nasty and scared thoughts to go away.

Ring. Ring. Ring.

Picking up the phone to see my sister's name on the display screen, I slid my thumb across and said, "Hello" before I put the phone to my ear.

"Hey, wanna grab some breakfast with me?"

"Maybe next time. I'm headed to breakfast with Casey."

"Ooo, where to?" she asked excitedly.

"His house."

Caught Up in a D-Boy's Illest Love

There was a brief silence before she started yelling, "My shy sister finna get that pussy bust open!"

Not in the mood for her jokes, I hung up the phone. Wasn't anyone going to burst shit of mines open! Driving away from my home, I listened to the automated voice tell me which way to turn out off my street.

For six minutes, I was a quiet, scared zombie in the front seat. Soon as I pulled into Casey's front yard, I was a nervous wreck as I didn't know what to expect from the two of us. After counting to fifty, I exited my car. Before approaching the porch, the stench of food cooking filled the air, which made my stomach growl.

I hope his cooking is as delicious as it smells, I thought while reaching towards the doorbell. Before I could press it, Casey was opening the door with a wide smile on his face.

"'Bout time you arrived, Ms. Lady."

"Sorry, I'm late," I stated quickly as I stepped inside of his cozy, warm home.

"Jonsey, I know you aren't nervous?" he inquired as he closed the door behind me.

"A little," I said before I knew it.

Caught Up in a D-Boy's Illest Love

"I'm going to be on my best behavior," he replied before turning me around and gently shoving me against the wall; his mouth was on mines within seconds.

Break away, I told myself as I reciprocated the passionate kiss he rendered to me. Trying to get a hold on things, I physically couldn't move my body as it disobeyed my mind. Casey lightly massaged my hands while his tongue and lips massaged mine.

My hands had a mind of their own as I tried to stop them from slowly creeping towards the sides of his face. The kiss deepened, and he pressed our bodies closer together, which I felt the huge bulge in the front of his black, gym shorts. *God, please intervene. I don't want to make a mistake again,* I prayed as I felt my pants unbuttoning. The tingling sensation was back in full throttle as my clit was begging to be touched. Within a split second, Casey's hand found its way inside of my panties, causing me to groan in his mouth. His thumb found my clit as a finger, followed by another finger, found the inside of my hot, wet pussy.

"Casey," I whined as he gently stroked me.

Caught Up in a D-Boy's Illest Love

"Do you want me to stop?" he asked while hungrily staring into my eyes and stroking my pussy faster, causing me to pant more instead of answering him.

"Jonsey, do you want me to stop?" he repeated himself again while nibbling on my bottom lip.

"No," I cooed as I placed my right hand on top of the hand he had in my panties.

Enjoying the thrusts his fingers were rendering to me, Casey started leaving trails of kisses from my lips down below all the while pulling my jeans down to my ankles. With his left hand, he removed my right shoe and pulled my leg out of that pants leg. Wanting to tell him that I didn't want us to go any further, the words never left my mouth. With a quick push of my right leg on his shoulder, I whimpered soon as his thick, long, wet, warm tongue slid into my pussy.

"Oh, my, Godddd!" I cooed loudly.

All the thoughts I had in my mind were no longer present as Casey took his precious time tasting and exploring my pussy. I was on the break of exploding when he removed his mouth and fingers away from my vagina. With the look of lust in his eyes, Casey picked me up and carried me to the sofa. I was ready for whatever he was going to serve me. His mouth game had me gone, and I surely didn't want to come back from that wonderful bliss.

Once I was on the sofa, Casey slid off my other shoe and my pants. That man went crazy as he dove his mouth and fingers inside of me. My coos, pleas, whimpers, and groans sounded off as he smacked, sucked, and licked on me. I don't know how long it was before he stopped tasting me, but I wanted to beg him to fuck me.

With a look of satisfaction on his face, he replied, "I think it's time for you to eat before your first class, right."

"Umm..."

Laughing, he said, "Ain't no umm, you got class in thirty minutes. You gotta clean yourself, eat, and be on your way to class."

"Thirty minutes?" I asked in a high-pitched voice.

"Yep," he laughed louder as his hands twitched, and I highly believe that he wanted to dive them and his mouth back on me.

"You telling me that we spent all that time...umm..."

"Yep."

Caught Up in a D-Boy's Illest Love

Not wanting to leave him with a throbbing pussy that was ready for him, I laid on the sofa saying, "Fuck class today. I wanna stay with you."

"Nope. I'm not going to be the reason why you skip school. Get up, clean yourself, eat, and then get that ass to school, Jonsey."

Extremely pissed, which I let him know, I gave up trying to argue with him that the first day really wasn't important. Fifteen minutes before my first class was to start, Casey was feeding me as I tried to take my time on leaving his home.

"Now, you are done eating. Go to school. Call me in between your classes," he replied sexily but sternly as he picked me up and carried me to my car.

Finally defeated, I was dragging my ass to ASU. Pissed at going with a wet, tingling pussy, I knew the time was going to come when I was going to get him back. Once on the school grounds, I ran to my first class.

Once I plopped my ass in the first available chair, I noticed that I wasn't the only one late as I heard, "My, my, my. Where shall I sit?"

My once sex-craved body was gone upon hearing Sebastian's silky voice. Anger soared in me immediately as I wondered, *what the fuck? Why is this bastard in this class? Damn it!*

Several thirsty broads in the room said, "You can sit by me, sexy."

Ain't this 'bout a half of a bitch, I angrily thought as I slammed my chemistry and notebook on the freshly cleaned, white table.

***

As soon as school was over, Jonzella said that it was a party going on at Club Freeze, and that she had to be in attendance. Before we left the house, Jonzella prepared us three shots of the Seven Deadly Sins, so I was feeling bubbly and warm inside—which Jonzella would have said that I was tipsy if she knew I was bubbly and warm.

At ten o'clock p.m., we sauntered through the noisy packed club, aiming for the bar. Standing behind some tall, light-skinned guys, Jonzella tapped their shoulders. Briefly speaking to both of them, they stepped aside at the same time she grabbed my wrists and pulled us in front of them. A rapid thank you left her lips before she placed our drink orders.

Soon as we received our drinks, we slid through numerous bodies in front of the bar, leading to the

Caught Up in a D-Boy's Illest Love

dance floor. The females went crazy as Gucci Mane's voice blasted from the speakers, "Shawty got an ass on her," which caused me to wind my body to the beat.

Females up close and afar were jamming along to the song. Slightly turning around, Jonzella was swaying her body from left to right with her cup to her lips. As I lightly danced, I scanned the packed club. There were so many people in the large-sized building that I knew without a doubt that some mess could pop off. I wanted to make sure that Jonzella and I were in the clear if anything happened. The last time we visited Club Freeze, I was very thankful nothing happened. Hopefully, this time it would remain the same way.

By the end of Gucci Mane's twerking song, I smelled the familiar scent, and my body went crazy. Images from earlier this morning appeared, and immediately, I was ready to spread my legs for him. My breathing became erratic as my fingers twitched. I grew weak in the knees as I remembered the flickers of tongue and the thrusts of his fingers.

My god, where he at? I thought as the beat dropped to "Say I Yi Yi" by Ying Yang Twins. I didn't want to seem nervous, anxious, or thirsty; therefore, I inhaled and exhaled several times before taking a gulp of the remaining concoction of my Seven Deadly Sins drink. As I brought the cup to my side, Casey was smiling in my direction with his eyes planted on me. He was to the left of me in a crowd of dark-skinned guys, whom all had blunts or cigarettes to their mouths with a plastic cup in one hand and a liquor bottle in the other.

My eyes never left Casey's as his didn't leave me. My pussy was on the verge of running away from me, and I wasn't mad at all. A part of me wanted to be bold and tell him let's blow this place, but I couldn't get my legs to move. Giving him a polite, but sexy, wave with a smile, I made sure not to seem to thirsty for him. Granted I should have been after the performance with his mouth earlier today.

"Oooh, bitch, I see Casey has his eyes all over you. You aren't acting nervous...what happened this morning?" Jonzella yelled in my ear.

Life happened Jonzella, life, I thought before responding with, "We had breakfast and enjoyed each other's company as usual."

"Is that all?" she probed.

"Yep," I lied.

Caught Up in a D-Boy's Illest Love

"Well, he hasn't stopped looking yet. So, go over and say hello to him, and then bring your ass back here. Don't do no lingering around or none of that shit."

Shaking my head at her comment, I continued dancing along to the song. I was on cloud nine, and I loved it when he sought me instead of me seeking him. It worked better for my ego.

"Why not?" she inquired, working my last damn nerve.

"Because I don't want to. We spoke to each other already, in case you weren't paying attention," I replied quickly before I scooted away from the wall which was near the dance floor. I didn't look to see if my sister was behind me because I knew that she was. As we made our way through the crowd, I felt eyes on me, but I wouldn't dare look to see who had their peepers on me. I secretly prayed it was Casey and that soon he would be standing either behind or beside me.

The DJ must've known that the liquor was talking to me when he mixed in "Handsome and Wealthy" by Migos. I lost it all and joined in the trio as they rapped. By the second verse, the smell of *him* crept further into my nostrils—along with the smell of strong weed. My heart rate sped, and I was panting for air.

Caught Up in a D-Boy's Illest Love

Lord, please don't let me have a panic attack in this club. How would that look? I thought as I felt his strong hands wrapping around my petite waist.

I need those hands a little bit lower, please, I yelled in my head.

"You know I've had my eyes on you for a while, Ms. Lady," his deep, thick southern voice spoke loudly in my ear.

Ready to play along with his little game, I turned around to face him—damn near about to faint because of my nerves. Before I let my nerves and horniness get the best of me, I said into his left ear, "Is that so?"

"Yes, it is," he replied before showing me those eleven golds I loved seeing.

"That's nice to hear."

Playing hard to get was my best quality, but now I shouldn't have played that card. Soon as I thought about what I was doing, it brought about a sense of excitement and naughtiness up front. Jonzella told me on several occasions that she and Totta role played while out in public, and it turned out to be wonderful once their clothing was off.

"Do you have a man?" he continued on in role play mode.

Caught Up in a D-Boy's Illest Love

As I shook my head, I asked, "Do you have a woman?"

"Nope. That ship sunk some months ago."

It better or you weren't going to have one peaceful night in Montgomery, Alabama, I thought as I gazed into his medium-sized, dark brown eyes and mouthed, "Good".

My hands were no longer shaky or sweaty as I planted them on his broad shoulders and glared into his eyes. It was time for me to put on my big girl draws and talk to the one man that made me weak at my knees. The same man that makes me smile whenever I see him. The one man that literally made me beg for him to sex me this morning.

He was about to open his mouth, but the bullshit popped off, which sealed his lips. Gunshots rang, liquid was being spilled, and people began running and screaming. In one swift move, I was scooped into Casey's arms. Ducking my head as low as I could, I scanned the small area to see where Jonzella was. In front of me, she was secured in the arms of Totta. Fear was still in my body until we were outside of the club.

"Aye, Dank, you good?" Totta yelled from in front of us, slowing down to stop at Jonzella's car.

"Yeah!" he replied while slowing down behind my sister's vehicle.

"Jonsey, are you okay?" my sister asked in a worried tone.

"Yeah, I'm good," I voiced lightly.

"I'mma need for y'all to get in the car and go, Jonzella," Totta's deep baritone voice spoke sternly to my sister.

"Tell your sister to go to IHOP by Atlanta Highway. We can finish our conversation there," Casey demanded as he put me on the ground.

"Okay," I replied in a scared tone as I nodded my head.

The chaos from inside found its way outside, and the always smiling guy that I was used to seeing was not smiling anymore.

"That's why I hate going out. These motherfuckers don't know how to act. Aye, Ms. Lady, y'all need to go. Go to where I told you too," Casey voiced sternly as he looked at me with a raised eyebrow.

"Okay," I replied to him as I looked at Jonzella and spoke clearly to her. "Let's get in the car and go."

Within a flash, we were safely inside of her car. Jonzella backed out of the parking spot and sped across the large parking area. While she drove, I was looking behind at the scene that Casey and Totta were in. Immediately, I prayed for his safety and that he would be leaving soon.

"Umm, bitch, what was said?" Jonzella questioned curiously.

Smiling and tucking my behind in the passenger's seat, I replied giggling, "We role played."

"So, you did take my advice and stepped out of the norm?"

"Actually, he kicked it off and I played along."

The short ride to IHOP went in a blur as Jonzella and I talked about Casey and Totta. Pulling into the parking lot of the restaurant, I was ecstatic since I was eager to finish the role play with Casey, and he could finally bless me with those fat, long inches of dick. Fifteen minutes of being inside of the busy establishment, our guys planted their bodies in the booth with us.

"Now, where were we, Ms. Lady?"

Feeling out of sorts with role playing in front of my sister and his homeboy, I nervously said, "I'm not quite sure."

"Ahh, yes. I think we'll pick that up after we eat," he deeply voiced while staring at me.

We were carrying on a nice conversation until we heard, "Mane, fuck that nigga. I'll air this bitch out! I have no problems with catching another murder case!

Caught Up in a D-Boy's Illest Love

Ain't naan finna talk crazy about my brother, and he dead."

Immediately, Casey and Totta hopped up and disappeared to where the angry man was located, which was at the entrance door.

Soon as they approached the man, everyone in IHOP heard them say, "You gon' have to leave, woe. You can't come up in these folk's place and start shit. Them White folks gon' hem yo' dumb ass up!" I saw Casey pushing the dude out of the lobby as Totta was shaking his head.

"Fuck that! He got his pussy ass up here...talking all that shit on Facebook...tell that nigga to come out this doe!"

"Let me get out of here. That nigga, Tron, ain't bullshitting. I got seven churren at home. There's no way in hell he finna air this motherfucker out with me in it," a chick stated in a matter-of-fact tone as she rushed to gather her keys, cell phone, and purse.

"Bitch, I think we need to go, also. Tron is Colt's older brother, and from what I've heard, he's 'bout that life. Anyone that is crazy enough to piss him off is seeking a death certificate. Bitch, I can't get no bomb dick in hell," Jonzella stated seriously as she grabbed her keys.

Caught Up in a D-Boy's Illest Love

While I laughed at her comment, I saw several people exiting the building while I was still stuck to the booth's seat. It took Casey to yell, "Aye, Ms. Lady, I need y'all to go home now. I'll call you once we get my cousin calm."

Nodding my head, I jumped from the table with a disappointed look on my face.

"I promise you I'll make it up to you. Right now, family calls me. I hope you understand."

"I do," I replied before strolling out of IHOP with Casey and Jonzella close by me.

Damn it. It's always an idiot fucking up something, I thought as Casey walked me to Jonzella's car as Totta was holding the dude, Tron, against Casey's vehicle.

Before I slipped inside of Jonzella's front seat, Casey whispered in my ear, "I'm hungry, Jonsey. I hope you are planning on feeding me."

Immediately, my body began to tingle as a shy smile across my face before I replied, "I sure will."

Chapter 11
Dank

As if a nigga didn't have enough on my plate, I had to rescue Tron from doing something stupid. I would've never heard the end of it from my folks if I didn't. He had already shown his ass at Club Freeze. I had to know what had him so riled up.

"Mane, what the fuck wrong with you, dude?" I yelled at him as I slid my body inside of my car.

"Shid, you know I'on fuck with nobody, Dank. That nigga, Mark, got it coming. Ain't no way he gon' test me like that," he voiced angrily as he removed his Glock from the back of his pants.

"Dude, you need some of that good good," Totta laughed as he handed Tron a blunt.

"Or some...he sure as hell just put a pause on my action," I replied somewhat angrily while shaking my head.

"That Facebook beef between you and Mark childish as fuck. Be the bigger man and cease that mess, Tron," Totta informed him seriously.

Caught Up in a D-Boy's Illest Love

As I started the engine, Tron was about to say something until my phone began to ring. Soon as I saw who was calling me, I sighed heavily before answering the phone.

"Didn't I tell you to stop calling my phone, guh?"

"I want you, Dank. We should've never broken up," Diamond stated in a whiny voice.

"Well, I don't know what to tell you other than I don't want you."

"Is it because of that thin bitch that you were hugged up on in Club Freeze tonight?" she asked with an attitude.

Not in the mood to argue with a peasant, I hung up the phone.

"Crazy broad?" Totta questioned before laughing.

"Fuck yeah," I replied as I slid down Atlanta Highway, heading for Lee Oaks.

"What in the hell was you thinking about fucking with that ugly duckling anyways?" my cousin laughed before exhaling.

"Hell, I had some gorgeous broads on my team that wasn't right in the dome. Then I jumped to the pretty to okay broads and they weren't about shit, so it was time for a nigga to try an ugly duckling. Plus, she caught me at a vulnerable time."

"If you say so," my cousin chuckled, which made all of us laugh.

"What was her momma thinking about naming her Diamond anyways?" Totta questioned seriously, which caused me to burst out laughing until tears seeped down my face because I knew where the conversation was heading.

"Soon as she came out the pussy she should've known she wasn't a damn diamond. More like an Aye-aye," Tron shrieked, causing my laughter to continue as the sight of an Aye-aye flashed in my head.

"Nigga, you stupid as fuck. Dank, drop this nigga off at home for that comment," Totta snickered as he slapped the dashboard.

I could barely see the road for the tears that were in my eyes. My stomach was hurting from laughing so hard at his comment and the visual images of the strangest looking creature in the world. Tron was just like Colt when it came to joking. He would have you out of breath before you knew it. Instantly, I wished that Colt was in the backseat, joking and laughing with us.

Caught Up in a D-Boy's Illest Love

"I'm not going home. Y'all can drop me off at my baby mama's crib," my heavy voiced family member voiced nonchalantly as he shuffled in the backseat.

"Boy, you wild. I'm not finna take you over that crazy broad's house. You need to lay low off that pussy right there. She gon' have you in prison, woe," I voiced seriously to the hardheaded individual as my laughter died down.

"No, it won't," he replied defensively.

Not in the mood to tell a grown man what to do, I shook my head. They started conversing while I thought about why Tron was still creeping around with Marleesha. She was the type of broad that loved to be in drama and didn't have anything going for herself. Those types of broads never caught my eye much less a hey.

I caught the end of their conversation as Totta said, "I'm finna go lay up with Jonzella."

"I kinda figured that," I voiced in a low tone.

"You better link up with her sister. From what was told to me, lil' mama wanting you. So, without a doubt, she'll drop them panties. I'on know why you be playing peek-a-boo with the pussy dude. Shid, that's all you want to do anyways is fuck...so fuck, my nigga," Totta stated seriously.

Caught Up in a D-Boy's Illest Love

Bursting out laughing at that fool, I replied, "Mane, ain't nobody playing peek-a-boo with Jonsey's pussy. We just be coolin'. Plus, I'm taking my time with her since you sent Jap to the restaurant some weeks back and fucked up that bet," I voiced blankly with a smirk on my face as I glanced at my partner, ignoring the fact that he was right about me wanting to sex her. I was tempted to, but I wanted it to be on my terms; since I had to figure out what I really needed her for.

"No wonder y'all keep getting done wrong...y'all be playing with these broads," Tron said in a matter-of-fact timbre.

"It's best to play with their minds first, or they will get you. Not naan will get me. I don't have time for that," Totta replied, which caused Tron and him to engage in a serious conversation about relationships and women.

Ignoring them, I pulled into my grandmother's yard and shut off the engine. It was one o'clock in the morning, and I wasn't ready to go home. Honestly, I didn't mind lying underneath Jonsey. Truth be told, ole girl was a breath of fresh air for me. I didn't have to think about the more pressing issues if I was with her.

With my phone in my hand, I dialed her number. My call went straight to voicemail. Quickly in my feelings, I sent her a text informing her to call me soon as she could. I stared at the phone for at least three minutes hoping she was going to call or respond. I was growing impatient as I waited for her to hit me up.

I was completely in the zone when Totta and my cousin said, "Aye, we gon' holla at cha later, woe."

"Aye, Tron, before you leave. What did Mark say that had you ready to spaz out?" I inquired, thinking back to his earlier statement about something Mark said on Facebook about Colt.

"Mane, that fuck nigga running around talking about Colt was getting fucked and fucking Baymatch on top of fucking with Mark's baby mama," he stated, growing angry at the mention of the situation.

It seemed as the wind was knocked out of my chest when he spoke; thus, me coughing to hide the look that I gave Totta. With a blank expression on his long, oval, black face, Totta cocked his head and looked at me. I didn't know what to say other than, "You know folks always got something to say. In that case, I should've let you whoop that nigga's ass. Next time you see him, you better whoop that ass on site."

Totta agreed with me as Tron said, "Damn, right."

Caught Up in a D-Boy's Illest Love

"I won't hold y'all up any longer. Be safe. Text me when y'all make it to your destination," I told them as I dapped them up, followed by reclining the seat back and finishing thinking about the brown skin creature that hadn't called or texted me.

Dick on brick mode, I was ready to fuck some and just not anything. I wanted to do some nasty, breathtaking things to Jonsey. The longer I sat in my grandmother's yard and glared at my phone, the more pissed off I got at her for not returning my call. Her entertaining another nigga never crossed my mind because I knew she wasn't the type to deal with more than one at a time. However, the thought did cross my mind—which caused me to call her phone. Twenty minutes of waiting for a call, I gave up and left my grandmother's home.

"I'm gon' punish her ass for not calling me back," I said aloud as I started the engine.

Ring. Ring. Ring.

Grabbing my phone from my lap, a nigga was smiling. *'Bout time,* I thought as I slid my finger across the answer button. My feelings were on one-thousand as I held a wide smile.

"'Bout time you call me back," I said smiling.

Caught Up in a D-Boy's Illest Love

"Aww, look at him. Sweating out my phone call," she sweetly replied in an innocent timbre.

Laughing, I replied, "Mane, go 'head with that. What are you doing, Ms. Lady?"

"Wrapped up in my towel and laying back on my bed. Come over," she replied quickly. Immediately, I imaged her little body snuggled inside of a white towel.

Dick super hard from the image, I quickly said, "Text me the address. I haven't left my grandmother's street yet."

"In that case, head down McQueen Street and make that left on Oliva Drive. Turn into the second duplex driveway on the left-hand side. You'll see Totta's truck outside. Park by his truck."

"A'ight," I replied before we hung up the phone.

Following the directions she gave me, I was at her crib in less than twenty seconds. Soon as I turned off the engine, that inner voice of mine told me not to go inside of her crib. Of course, I didn't listen; I knew when to cut things off between us before it got too far. Exhaling heavily, I hopped out of my whip and strolled towards the porch where my partner and Jonzella were sitting, chief'ing on that good good.

"Got that gas in the air," I sang.

"Yep, you wanna hit?" Totta questioned.

"Nawl, I'm good," I told him before I briefly became acquainted with Jonzella since I didn't get a chance to do that when I first saw her.

Disappearing into the nicely decorated and wonderful smelling duplex, Jonsey greeted me with a bright grin on her face as she wore the hell out of a white ASU t-shirt, green gym shorts, and mixed matched ankle socks.

"Welcome to Jonzella's and my home," she happily stated as she motioned for us to take a seat on the short, gray and black sectional.

Soon as Jonzella and Totta strolled in, the conversations and drinks began. Those women could drink their asses off. I had to tap out with the drinks, given I wasn't a drinker but a smoker. Eventually, Totta tapped out as well. I had to say that they were different than any broads that Totta and I used to fuck around with. I could tell that Jonzella was more street smart than her sister, which was cool with me.

As I observed the women in their natural habitat, my thoughts fell on what I was going to do with Jonsey. After deciding that she deserved better than what I had to offer her, I knew immediately that I had to fuck and leave her alone. It wasn't like she didn't want the dick, anyways. From the moment I put my mouth on Jonsey, she was all ball for whatever I was going to serve her. One would say that I was scared of commitment, and they would be right; however, I knew that I had some serious things going on in my life, and she didn't need to be involved in it. She was a good girl; the type to knock up and wife, and I wasn't sure if those things would happen, yet.

Fuck and leave, I thought while she looked at me with a sex-crazed facial expression as Totta and Jonzella told us goodnight.

"Night," Jonsey and I replied in unison.

Upon the closing of a door down the hallway, Ms. Lady questioned in a slurred tone, "Can we finish what you started?" Her tongue grazed my ear, which made a tingling sensation run down my spine.

"I'on know about all that. You are drunk, woman. I want you sound mind when you get this dick," I laughed while enjoying the tricks she was rendering my ear.

"I know the big bad Casey isn't scared of the shy Jonsey," she voiced as she sat in my lap.

"Nawl, just don't want to fuck up your life with this dick," I announced as I glared into her eyes as my dick pressed against her hot pussy.

Caught Up in a D-Boy's Illest Love

Chapter 12
Jonsey

My head was spinning from the shots we took. My words were slurred, my pussy was super wet, and my body was craving for Casey to touch it. My ladylike morals disappeared once I couldn't control my thoughts or actions. Before I knew it, him and I were naked in my bed as the music played at a nice decibel from the radio's speakers in Jonzella's room.

The lining of my body was set on fire by his soft hands, delicately trailing it. Running my hands through his hair, I cooed at his tender touches and silently rushed for him to enter me. This moment was what I dreamt of for so long; for it to finally be realistic was one amazing feeling. As the bright moon light lit up my room, I had a content, yet frustrated, expression across my face while I welcomed his lean body in between my legs as he began to suck on my neck.

"Mmphm," I groaned as he bit down a little harder on my tingling neck.

Tired of the soft foreplay, I decided that it was time to amp things up a bit. I had waited long enough for him to pursue me. It was time for me to take matters into my own hands. Pushing him onto his back, I stated, "You've done enough kissing on me. Time for me to return the favor. By the way, I love chocolate."

"Oh, you do, huh?" he chuckled as he popped my butt.

"Yep," I seductively responded in his ear as I blew, licked, and sucked on it.

"Umm," he groaned aloud.

While sucking on his ears and gently rubbing his neck, I ran my hands down his body until I had his long, fat pole in my warm, petite hands. *My, my, my, what an interesting pole he has,* I thought as a huge grin spread across my face. I've always hoped that he didn't have a massively fat and long dick, but once the tension grew between the two of us—I simply didn't care anymore. I was going to take what was given to me. I was going to have to deal with a big dick, granted it was horrible for the pussy walls. Immediately, I grimaced at the thought of how the pain would be present since I hadn't had sex in a year.

"You okay, Ms. Lady? We don't have to do anything," Casey voiced lowly.

Caught Up in a D-Boy's Illest Love

"Yes, I'm fine, and we are going to do this. What you did to me yesterday against your wall and sofa was wonderful, yet you wouldn't give me the rest of you."

"You in charge. Whenever you want to stop, just say so," he voiced calmly as he rubbed my thighs, which ignited a pure passionate firestorm inside of my soul.

As excitement ran through me, I started trailing my tongue from the center of his chest downwards. I knew what glorious pleasures were going to be rendered upon us. I was going to have a little trouble sucking his dick, but five minutes of getting my gag reflexes in check on top of fifteen minutes of getting my throat muscles together, that task would be complete. My goal was to down at least six to seven inches within the first three minutes of having his penis in my mouth.

Landing my tongue on the head of his dick, I slowly rotated my head from left to right, all the while letting my mouth become soaking wet with saliva.

"Got damnnn," he groaned as he placed his hand on the back of my head.

My body relaxed as I enjoyed sucking on Casey. As I went to town on his chocolate stick, I knew that I was getting ready to snatch his soul from his body. The liquor was talking to me, telling me that I could reach for the stars, and that was my goal! If he thought he had received the best head in the world, he was sadly mistaken. I wasn't going to waste my time or his! I was going to give him what he deserved from me—some royal loving from a real lady.

Jacquees "Won't Waste Your Time" was playing as I showed out with my mouth piece. I had to let Casey know that whenever he was in my presences there would never be a dull time.

"You gotta come from down there, Jonsey...my God," he moaned as one of his hands played with my nipples while the other softly rubbed my ear.

"Are you sure?" I asked, sucking on the head of his lollipop.

"Yes...no...yes," he replied indecisively.

Doing as he wished, I reached in my drawer to hand him a condom. Shaking his head, he replied, "I got my own."

"Cool," I responded, feeling somewhat offended. However, I let it slide. As I watched him put on the condom, I was sucking on his balls while massaging them.

"Fuck," he whimpered as his hands began to tremble.

"You like that?" I cooed, looking up at him.

"Yes," he replied, holding out the s in yes.

Within seconds of it being on, I continued to fondle and slobber on his sagging balls.

"I want my dick in you now, Jonsey," he voiced while grabbing me by my thighs and gently laying me at the bed. Engaged in a sweet, overheated tongue kiss while fingering me, Casey rubbed the head of his rubber coated dick against my begging clit.

"Mmm," I groaned as my body felt as if it was electrocuted.

"You ready?" he mumbled against my lips, further pressing his fingers towards my G-Spot.

"I think s—" I tried to coo while he slowly moved his fingers out of me.

Shortly after, I jumped back a little from the discomfort of him trying to shove his dick inside of me. Causing me to say, "It's been a while."

"What is a while?" he asked curiously as he inserted his fingers back inside of me, gliding for my G-Spot.

"Thirteen months, per se," I replied as my body was responding to the delicate thrusts of his fingers.

After he got my body to the desired wetness, he slid inside. There wasn't pain, but I surely was uncomfortable for a while, until I got somewhat used to

173

his length and girth. Casey was extraordinary when it came down to the way he took care of my non-fucking pussy. That was a plus in my eyes. When I could take what he was giving me, we gave my bed a helluva show; one that left me eager for more of him as we continued to please each other's bodies.

"You got some bomb bomb, Ms. Lady," he lowly whimpered as I slowly rode him while talking nasty to him.

Loving the praises he was giving me, I went the extra mile to make my muscles suck him. Kegels was a very important tool to use during sex, and I used the hell out of them. It was a for sure way to get any man hooked on your goods, and that was my goal for Casey!

"Fuckk!" he called out while he began to roughly slam his dick inside of me.

"Oouuuu, Caseeey!" I screamed out in pleasure. The pain was present, but it didn't stop me from feeling wonderful sensations from our sexing.

"I'on want you fucking nobody, understood?" he demanded as he banged my back loose.

My mission complete, I thought as I moaned, "Yessss."

Close to my climax, my body began to shake uncontrollably; thus, bringing Casey to slowly deep stroke me. Before I knew it, my body became extremely hot as my juices and screams sounded off.

"Cassseeeyyy...this dick great."

"I know," he snickered while still pumping inside of me.

One round turned into two and two turned into three before I passed out—extremely satisfied.

***

"Bitch, it's three o'clock in the afternoon...get cho' ass up," Jonzella voiced as the sun's rays blasted through my room.

"I'm tired. Go away, heifer," I griped.

"Hell no, I'm not. Bitch, we finna gossip. You were turning up in this mother mother this morning," she laughed.

Wanting to be mad at her for interrupting my rest, I couldn't. Instead, I grinned and shook my head at her.

"There's nothing to talk about, Jonzella. Geesh, you know you be making a big deal out of nothing."

"You've been dreaming of the day of you and him, and now it's in the happening, so I want to know how are you feeling?"

Caught Up in a D-Boy's Illest Love

"Amazing, chick, amazing. Now, get out so I can get myself together."

After she left my room, I quickly grabbed my cell phone to see did Casey text or call me. I was highly disappointed as I didn't have either from him. Quickly shoveling the negative thoughts to the back of my head, I brought forward the positive ones as I climbed out of my bed. Still naked, I ran into the bathroom. Turning on the shower, I felt my pussy pulsating. I haven't had sex in over a year, so my body was letting me know exactly how much "fun" I really had with Casey.

Jumping in the shower, I had a smile on my face as I rehashed the moments between him and me. Nothing and no one could take the joy away that I was feeling from being in his presence. One thing I knew for certain was that I was hooked on that nigga! I had to be his one and only; I wasn't going to have it any other way.

After my shower, I ambled to the kitchen. Upon opening the fridge, I pulled out leftovers from Tuesday as Jonzella was yelling, "Trick, your cell phone ringing."

Quickly placing the food on the white kitchen counter, I ran to my room, hoping that Casey was calling me. Seeing his name on the screen had me smiling and happy as ever. Answering the phone as normal as I could, I plopped on my unmade bed.

"Hello."

"Good afternoon, Ms. Lady. How are you?" he asked sweetly in his deep voice.

"Afternoon. I'm good and you?"

"Good. What you got planned for tonight?"

"Nothing. What's up?" I smiled as I happily thought about us ransacking my bed again.

"I wanna chill with you. I'll bring over some movies."

"That's cool. What would you like to eat?"

"We'll eat out. Is that cool?"

"Yes," I voiced happily as I pumped my fist in the air several times.

"Is six o'clock cool for me to come over?"

"Yes, it is."

"Okay. I'll see you then. Have a good day, Ms. Lady."

"Same to you," I replied before we ended the call.

Screaming loudly, I startled Jonzella.

"What in the fuck is wrong with you, nut basket?" she yelled as she ran into my room.

"Food and movies tonight at six with Casey ... here."

With a blank look on her face, Jonzella slapped her hands on her hips and said, "Bitch, you should've dated more when you were a teenager. You don't know how to act."

"Shut up," I laughed as I threw a pillow at her.

"Be careful with your feelings, okay?" she stated sincerely.

Confused at why she would say that, I asked, "Why do you say that?"

"True enough, you've seen him a thousand times since we've been staying in the neighborhood. Yes, y'all have been courting or whatever you call it, but you still need to be mindful that y'all are not dating. Don't be so clingy and make sure to give him space. See, what he's *really* like before you fall head over heels for him. Most importantly, make sure that he has the same type of feelings that you possess. The last thing you want to do is put too much energy into a person that isn't giving you that same energy."

"Gotcha," I replied rapidly before she waltzed out of my room.

Ring. Ring. Ring.

Looking down at my phone, I smiled lightly at my mother's name displaying across the screen.

"Hello, Mommy," I sang as I answered her call.

Caught Up in a D-Boy's Illest Love

"Well, hello darling. Haven't heard from my lovely daughters in a couple of days. How's work and school?"

"Both are good. I don't know about Jonzella, but I'm ready for another break."

"Well, your father and I we will start discussing things to do for spring break. Of course, we'll get you ladies' opinion on a nice family vacation we can take, if applicable."

What the hell 'if applicable' meant, I surely didn't know, and truth be told, I was scared to ask. Thus, I kept it simple since my stomach was growling.

"Okay. Keep us informed, Mom. Either Jonzella or I will tell you when we are out of school for spring break."

"Perfect. Speaking of Jonzella, where is she?"

"She's either in the kitchen or the front room."

"Okay. Tell her I said hello and that I love her."

"I will do," I stated quickly as my mother said, "That bitch, Renee Johnson, sought me on Facebook, inquiring about her. I had to tell her a thing or two about asking about my baby. She had my pressure so high that I had to block that worthless piece of crap."

"Mom, after all she is Jonzella's biological mother. I think you should tell her how well she's doing."

"Nope. It's none of her business. If she wanted to know the happenings of Jonzella, the bitch should've been the best mother to her. Instead, of chasing someone that didn't want her as a mother. I will not have her disrupting the wonderful life that Jonzella has. End of discussion."

"Mom," I tried to reason with her.

"Mom, nothing. Every two years, she trying to reach out. Nope, I'm not having anyone inconsistent in Jonzella's life, and I meant that."

My mom started doing breathing exercises, which informed me that she was growing pissed at the thought of Renee Johnson trying to weasel her way back into Jonzella's life. As the silence overtook my phone, I yelled to Jonzella that mother said hello and that she loved her.

Running into my room, my sister's high-pitched voice said, "Hello, Mommy. Me love you! Tell Dad hi, and that I love him."

Placing our mother on speakerphone, she loudly stated, "I sure will tell him. Tonight, I want to chat with both of you."

"Umm, around what time?" I asked curiously as Jonzella laughed at me.

"About seven."

Caught Up in a D-Boy's Illest Love

"Can it be before then?"

"Why?"

"I have a date tonight."

"With whom?" our mother probed.

"With a friend, mom."

"You better make sure he isn't with the bull crap. I hate to have to cut his dick off," she voiced sternly as Jonzella burst out laughing.

"Oh God, Mom. Trust you won't have to do that. He's a gentleman."

"Well, I guess we can chat some time tomorrow. What time do y'all work?"

"I work from nine to four, and Jonzella works from eight to five."

On Fridays, we had no school and a full schedule at work—which was fine with me. On the other hand, once I was off the clock, I would be studying or getting ahead on next week's assignment.

"Y'all call me when y'all get settled in."

"Okay. Love you, Mom," Jonzella and I stated in unison.

"Love y'all more."

After ending the call with my mother, I resumed to the kitchen to warm up my food as Jonzella and I talked about the two guys that had big smiles on our faces.

Caught Up in a D-Boy's Illest Love

Afterwards, we cleaned our home—vacuuming, sweeping, dusting, and making up our beds.

Before I knew it, time was approaching for my company to arrive, and my heart was beating rapidly. Thumbing through my clothes, I decided to wear a pair of denim shorts and a pink shirt. At 5:30 p.m., I was fully dressed and ready for my night to begin. Jonzella was strolling down the hallway, wearing a brown sweater, denim jeans, and brown booties. The brown on the booties and sweater complemented her dark brown skin. Gold hoop earrings were tucked into her earlobes and several gold bangles were on her left wrists.

"Sexy momma, where are you going?"

"Out to eat with Totta's crazy ass."

"Oh, snaps. Have a good time, and be careful."

"Always," she replied quickly and then she continued, "You enjoy your date with Eleven Golds...I mean Casey."

"And that I will," I replied before she waltzed out the door.

Time was ticking, and I couldn't wait until he was in my presence. My nerves were all over the place, and I was tired of feeling like I was going to have a panic attack. Looking at the DVR box, it read five fifty-seven. My thirsty ass was waiting for him like SSI and SSDI recipients were waiting on the first and the third of each month.

Ring. Ring. Ring.

Looking down at my phone, my heart was doing somersaults as his name displayed across the screen. Immediately, I hoped that he wasn't cancelling out date.

As casual as possible, I said, "Hello."

"I'm outside. Will you open the door for me, Ms. Lady?" he questioned pleasantly.

"My pleasure," I replied as I hopped off the sofa and opened the door for him with a huge grin on my face.

In his hands were two big bags from Jim-N-Nicks, flowers, and a big, brown bear. Seeing that dark-skinned man did numbers on my mental and body; not to mention, the items that I knew were for me. I wanted to jump his bones immediately, but I had to refrain from doing so.

Approaching the porch, he sweetly announced, "Food and gifts for you, Ms. Lady."

"Thank you," I replied, blushing.

Seeing him through the threshold of the door, I closed and locked it. As he took a seat on the sofa, I asked him was there anything that I needed to get from the kitchen.

"Nope. Let's eat and chill."

While eating, we talked. I wanted to know more about the man that had my panties in a bunch whenever I saw him, as he wanted to know more about me. We had so much in common that it was unbelievable; from liking sports to traveling to the way we thought about society to the African American community needing major help. We were meant to be together, and I surely wasn't going to entertain no one else.

"Time to get lost in some movies. What do you say Ms. Lady?"

"I agree," I stated as I held up his movie selections.

"You choose, Ms. Lady," he voiced seductively before licking his lips all the while holding my gaze.

Instantly, I lost it. I had my lips on his before he could blink his eyes. Our tongues collided together at the same time our hands roamed over each other's bodies.

Breaking the intense kiss and touches, Casey said, "No...no...we are going to watch these movies. We got time for all that other stuff later, Ms. Lady."

"Okay," I stated as I fake pouted.

"You gon' make a nigga—" he began to say while he shut his phone off.

"Make a nigga what?" I inquired with a funny smirk on my face.

"Put a movie on, woman," he laughed, flashing those eleven golds.

"My pleasure," I lightly voiced as I did what he commanded.

Knowing that I wanted some more of him, I took a seat, inches away from him. Mr. Casey wasn't hearing that. Roughly sliding me towards him, he spat, "If you don't get cho' ass close to me, I know something."

With a huge grin on my face, I slid close to him. Draping his left arm around me, he licked my ear before whispering, "Don't make me fuck you up!"

"What you talking about?" I asked in an astonished tone, but a sister was ecstatic that he was feeling the same way that I was.

"Just don't make me fuck you up."

"I won't," I replied as I snuggled further into his arm.

As the new version of *Beauty and The Beast* played, I was in La-La Land. The one movie I was dying to see, I couldn't focus. All I could think about was me having Casey in between my legs, followed by him and me making things official between the two of us. Then, the thoughts of the bet that he made came to the forefront of my head, and all I could think about was *is this part of another bet.* Trying everything in my power to change my drastically upset mood, I placed my thoughts on how he proved that he was sorry for what he did. *Casey is nothing like Sebastian,* I told myself several times before Casey spoke.

"Jonsey, I'm nothing like the other guys you've ever been with, am I?"

Damn, can he read minds? I thought as I turned around to look in his eyes, I replied, "Not sure. Never been the type to date."

"May I ask why?"

"In the past, it seemed that I attracted the egotistical, always in other females' faces, and just want to fuck and go on about their business type of dudes. Or they wanted to use me as they transported their dope in my book bag, tampon box, or whatever I was carrying— without my knowledge. So, after those fucked-up encounters I kept to myself until...you."

"You won't have to worry about that with me, Ms. Lady. If I'm fucking with you, I'm fucking with you only. Feel me?"

"Yes," I replied as I nodded my head.

Caught Up in a D-Boy's Illest Love

"Now, let's finish watching this girly ass movie. If I had known they would do all this singing, I would've never gotten it," he chuckled before planting a kiss on my neck.

"So, I'm assuming you never watched the cartoon version."

"I did, but hell I was a kid then. It never dawned on me that this shit would be the same as the cartoon," he voiced as he shrugged his shoulders.

Shaking my head with a naughty look on my face, I said boldly, "Well, we can skip the movie and do some grown up things."

"Watch the movie, Jonsey," he voiced sternly with a raised eyebrow and then continued, "This dick ain't going nowhere anytime soon … so trust you gon' get it."

Chapter 13

Dank

My original plan of dicking Jonsey down once, followed by leaving and putting her on the block list didn't go as I planned. Her mouthpiece was a beast, and I wasn't expecting it; that fire monkey between her legs was the type of pussy that I had no business dipping in—condom or not. The moment she told me that she hadn't had sex in thirteen months, I knew I was surely fucked.

Earlier this morning after the third round while she was sleeping, I left for a reason—to make her feel some type of way. Hell, I ended up leaving feeling some type of way. I tried my best to keep her from my thoughts, but she invaded it at every turn. Her personality alone had me all in. That was another reason why I knew I had to find a way to break free from her; I was hoping that she would do something that would turn me off. That's when the invite of us chilling came into play.

Halfway through the movie, I kept thinking about our sexual encounter and how she catered to my body. My dick was hard, and I didn't want to dive in her. Sex wasn't my goal for the night; it was finding a reason to put her on the block list. Into the second movie, I stopped focusing on finding that one flaw; I began to enjoy her company and the movie.

Maybe she is what I need in this thuggish life of mine. Maybe she is just the escape that I really need right now, I thought as she was lying in my arms.

"Now, it's my turn to ask you are you okay?"

"Yeah, Ms. Lady, I'm good. Why do you ask?"

"Because your body isn't relaxed."

Kicking off my shoes, I said, "Hold up for a sec. I want you to lay all the way on me."

Doing as I commanded, her smelling good, petite body was on top of me as we resumed watching TV. Thirty minutes into the movie, her cell phone rang. She ignored it, and immediately, that raised the red flag.

"You ducking and dodging some dude?" I tried to sound as if I was joking, but I was dead serious.

"Nope. I'm not entertaining anyone but you, Casey," she softly replied as she lifted her head and looked in my eyes.

"A'ight," I responded as her cell phone stopped ringing, only to start back sounding off.

"Uggh, let me get this," she stated in an annoyed tone as she lifted off me to retrieve her phone from the ground.

With her phone in her hand, she said loud and clear, "Kenneth Jameson Brown, what in the hell do you want blowing up my phone like that?"

Immediately, my ears were open, and my eyes never left her body.

Did she just call one of the niggas that told on me, Danzo, and Totta? This person must be someone else with the same name. Ain't no way this is the fuckboy that snitched on us, I thought as Jonsey continued talking on the phone.

"I have company, Kenny. I'll call you back," she stated quickly, calling her brother by the nickname Danzo has mentioned a time or two before.

Is it that nigga? I continued asking myself.

She laughed briefly before saying, "I'm grown. I can handle my own. Since you all in my business, when I call you back, we got some stuff to talk about. Like I said, when I call you back I want details. Now, bye."

On the verge of ending the call, the dude must've inquired about her sister because she replied with, "She's gone on a date, Kenny. Now, bye."

Caught Up in a D-Boy's Illest Love

The call was complete, and I had questions that I wanted answered immediately. I had to be very careful in how I asked them, as I didn't want to raise alarm.

"I'm sorry about that. That was one of my brothers calling and being a pest," she giggled, resuming into my arms at the same time she dropped her phone on the floor.

"No problem. I know how brothers can be. Tell me a little bit about your family," I asked curiously, trying to eliminate her brother from our kill list.

"My parents have been married for forty-five years, and they are retired from the Army. I have three older brothers, Kyvin is the oldest, we call him Ky. He's an engineer for a company called Boeing. Kevin is the second to the oldest, and he's somewhat of a problem child. He's trying to get his life together since the streets got ahold of him. Kenneth, aka Kenny, is the third child, and he's all over the place. My folks are loving and caring. My parents adopted Jonzella when she was seven years old. We are originally from Fort Lauderdale, Florida, but we moved to Prattville when I was nine. My parents and two of my brothers live in Myrtle Beach, South Carolina."

Caught Up in a D-Boy's Illest Love

Could it be a coincidence that the same niggas that's on our paperwork have the same names as the ones her brothers have? There are a million niggas by the name of Kevin Brown and Kenneth Brown. I need Kevin's middle name. That way I will know for sure. At least Totta and I got a location to look at, I thought as I voiced sincerely, "Hopefully, one day I will get the pleasure of meeting your family."

I couldn't wait until I talked with Totta; we had to get a handle on the situation quickly. The entire investigation would be over with soon as we get rid of the snitches that the DA didn't trust and was skeptical of using.

"I hope so," she softly replied before placing her mouth on mine.

My mind was on one thousand as I thought about the name that she called out when she was on the phone.

Could the dudes be the same people that we are looking for? If so, you need to pull away from this chick, I thought as Jonsey's kisses and the movie playing in the background didn't stop my mind from thinking of how quickly we were going to see if these niggas were the ones running their mouths. I prayed heavy that they weren't because a part of me didn't want to see Jonsey mourning. On the contrary, if they were the snitches, then their asses were good as dead. There was no way my peeps and I were going to be in anyone's prison cell. We did the streets of Montgomery a fucking favor, according to folks who were tired of those thieving young boys.

As she slid her hands up my shirt, I heard the front door handle roughly jiggling. On alert mode, I quickly grabbed my Glock from the back of my pants. In an instant, my weapon was off safety.

With her lips sucking on my neck and her hands continuing to probe further south, she calmly spoke, "Chill, chill. That's Jonzella."

"I gotta make sure," I replied nonchalantly with my eyes locked in on the front door.

"If y'all are naked, we are coming in," Jonzella's high-pitched voice stated through the crack of the door, causing my nerves to somewhat return normal as I flipped the gun back into safety position and laid it on the floor.

"We good," Jonsey chuckled.

Stepping in, Totta had a blank look on his face as Jonzella's face held happiness. *He knows something,* I thought as I analyzed my partner's face.

"Aye, Dank, I need to holla at cha fo' a minute," Totta's deep voice spat as he stood in front of the open door.

"Bet," I replied while Jonsey lifted off me.

Rapidly putting my shoes on, I shoved my gun into the back of my pants. Hopping off the sofa, I glanced at Jonsey and said, "I'll be right back, K?"

"K," she lightly replied as her eyes held hope and contentment.

I hope these niggas ain't your brothers, Ms. Lady. You are most definitely going to mourn for quite some time. On the other hand, wasn't I just looking for a way to dismiss her, I thought as I skipped out of the door, ensuring that it was tightly closed behind me.

Totta and I were quiet as we strolled towards his silver Yukon truck. Neither of us said a word until we hopped in his ride.

We spoke the same thing at the same time, "I believe them niggas that snitched on us is their brothers."

Shaking our heads, I offered him to speak first.

"Okay, so me and Jonzella were talking about our families and shit, right? So, she showed me a picture of her family. Immediately, I recognized the two niggas that we let go. Anyways, as she is showing me the pictures, she rattles off their names and ages. She even told me that they were troublemakers, and that they stayed in trouble since they were teenagers. And their parents put a tight leash around their necks since they recently got in trouble for something, which she doesn't know what."

"Myrtle Beach, South Carolina is where we need to be looking at," I huffed.

"What did you learn?" Totta asked as he fired up a blunt.

"Their names mostly, and that they live in Myrtle Beach. Jonsey didn't want to say anything since her and I was chilling. All of this started because of the nigga, Kenny, calling her phone. She called him by his full name. We have two options: one, hold the girls hostage and demand that the brothers show their faces, or two, play underneath the girls to get to the guys and off them niggas," I voiced seriously as Totta passed me the blunt.

"Shid, you know I'm down for whatever, woe. It don't make me none. As long as we ain't going to prison," Totta hissed as he inhaled the good good.

"We need to be heading to Myrtle Beach and cease them niggas from living. If need be, I'll reach out to J-Money and see about using his sharp shooter skills."

Caught Up in a D-Boy's Illest Love

Nodding his head as he inhaled his good good, Totta stated calmly, "You think he gon' want us to join The Savage Clique if we ask for his help?

"Nawl, he ain't that type of nigga. However, he likes to have his circle large as the former Queen pin did. A favor for a favor," I replied honestly as I thought of the perfect time to reach out to J-Money.

"A'ight. Well, I think we should play underneath the females. Never know when something could slip out of their mouths. One thing I do know is that Jonzella is completely dumb to our situation."

Nodding my head as I retrieved the blunt, I relaxed my body against the seat and prayed that everything would pan out right—that we would kill the snitches and that my partner and I weren't going to prison.

After we finished chief'ing, we waltzed into the crib. On the sofas were the beautiful cackling women. Seeming normal as we usually do, Totta and I had to know what had their mouths running one-hundred miles per hour.

"What y'all gossiping about, nih?" Totta asked in a joking manner as he slid his six-two, muscular body towards the long sofa, which Jonzella was outstretched on.

Caught Up in a D-Boy's Illest Love

"Your non-drinking self," Jonzella laughed.

"Mane, I do drink. I'm just not an alcoholic like you," he chuckled as he lightly popped her on the thigh before picking her up and placing her in his lap.

Taking a seat next to Jonsey, I glared at her. Her beauty was undeniable. From the light acne across her face to her big, brown pug-like eyes, they made your eyes stay on her face. Soft, long limbs with skinny, long fingers were perfect for grasping, touching, and sucking on. Pretty, short, manicured toes were soft and suck-able. Her brown, rounded face was perfectly shaped. Her medium-length hair was braided into box braids; I knew the length of her hair because I've been seeing her for three years—around our neighborhood.

"Why are you staring at me like that?" Jonsey inquired, interrupting my thoughts.

"I was observing your outside appearance," I responded casually.

My response made her blush and rub her hands across her face. Instantly, I knew that she was insecure about the way that she looked. It was my duty to make sure that she was comfortable in her own skin.

Caught Up in a D-Boy's Illest Love

"Aye, Ms. Lady, I didn't mean to make you feel any kind of way. You are beautiful, and don't let anyone tell you differently," I told her as slid closer to her body.

Nodding her head but ensuring not to look at me, Jonsey sighed heavily before lifting off the sofa.

"Where are you going?" I inquired, curiously.

"To take a shot of Jack D. Anyone down?" she replied, waltzing away.

"Meee," Jonzella yelled happily with her hands in the air.

"Damn drunks," Totta laughed, which caused all of us to burst out in laughter.

Minutes later, the girls took six shots to the head. I looked at Totta and nodded my head. In response, he nodded his head. The nodding of our heads meant that it was time to play underneath their asses and get as much information as we could so that we could set our plan in motion.

They put on a dancing show for us, which I surely loved. They could twerk their asses off; they were damn near better than the broads that twerked for a living. The show took a turn when they asked us to dance with them. I couldn't lie like I didn't have fun with them because I did.

Caught Up in a D-Boy's Illest Love

They were carefree and happy, and their vibes were what I needed; however, I still had to stay focused on the task at hand. The slow jams came about, and it was some nasty grinding going on, which led everyone to their prospective places—the bedroom.

The knocking of Jonsey's headboard began shortly after the oral sex session finished. Toe-curling sex, moaning, and groaning were in full effect. Great, dope dick was curving and slamming into great, wet pussy, which equaled a lot of cooed promises.

"Oh, my goddd! I don't want this to ever stop, Caassey," Jonsey groaned as I shoved my dick into the right corner of her pussy.

With a fist full of braids, I replied harshly, "Is that so?"

"Yessss," she whimpered as she arched her back.

"Who's...your...fucking...king?"

"Yooouuuuu!" she screamed from pure pleasure.

"Do I gotta compete with the next nigga?" I growled in her ear.

"Noo."

Slowing down my deep thrusts, I made love to her pussy. I knew what I had to do to get her extremely hooked on me; thus, me pulling out of her. Delicately placing her on her back, I opened her legs wide before diving my face into her hairless pussy. Knowing that I was a certified sloppy toppy doctor, I gave her peach scented pussy the business.

"If...you...ever...give...my...dick...and...mouth...away, nigga, I...will...fuck...you...up!" she cooed, pausing in between each word.

Yep, you almost at the crazy bitch stage. Let me sho' nuff get you where I want you at, I thought as I stuck two fingers inside of her. With my two fingers, I made them tap dance against her G-Spot as I held firmly yet softly on her small bud.

In a matter of seconds, she exploded on my fingers all the while loudly groaning, "My Cassseeyyy. I love youuuu!"

I got her ass now. She'll unass whatever I want in a heartbeat, I thought while sliding my tongue into her hole and sucking up her juices.

With a proud feeling, I knew that the rest of the night would go as *I* wanted it.

Chapter 14

Jonsey

The birds were chirping outside as the sun shined brightly through my ivory hued curtains. The smell of cooked bacon caused my eyes to open as my dry mouth began to salivate. With a frown on my face, I noticed that Casey wasn't in the bed.

Welp, I better get used to him leaving after we fuck, I thought quickly as I slid my naked behind out of my bed. Slowly walking towards my three-drawer dresser, I saw his low top, black Air Force Ones at the foot of my bed. Mood changing back to happiness, I rushed to open the first drawer and grabbed loungewear. With my clothing in my hand, my bedroom door opened as Casey spoke, "Time to eat, Ms. Lady."

"Okay," I replied as I held my loungewear in front of my naked body.

Planting his eyes on me, his chocolate ass started laughing. Looking at him like he lost his mind, with my eyebrow rose, I asked, "What are you laughing at?"

"If you don't put your hands down, I know something."

Caught Up in a D-Boy's Illest Love

"Umm, I'm naked," I replied in a shy timbre.

"As you were last night...we don' did everything under the sun...in your bed with no clothes on. Now, you wanna act shy and shit since my dick and mouth ain't on you," he replied casually as he shook his head, clearly hiding the laughter that was dying to come from his mouth.

With nothing to say, I waltzed into my closet and snatched my robe down. After I put the cozy attire on, Casey was in tears from laughing. I really didn't see anything funny. Needless to say, I was very shy. In my mind, there was a big difference between having sex with the lights off versus the sun showing off your body. Stomping past his ignorant behind, I had a severe smirk on my face. By the time I had my right leg over the door's threshold, I was in his arms while he rained kisses on my neck.

"Chill out, Ms. Lady. I was only joking with you. I know that you are shy and shit. You don't have to be around me. You want me to bathe you?" he asked sweetly against my neck.

"Umm, no, I can take care of that," I giggled, sinking further into his arms.

Caught Up in a D-Boy's Illest Love

"A'ight. Well, don't take too long. I'm not gonna eat without you," he strongly voiced while massaging my stomach.

Enjoying his strong hands on my body, I lightly whimpered. This moment and all the others were the ones I was dying for. Without a doubt, Casey and I were never going to end. I didn't care who tried to come in between us or how he conducted his business, I wasn't going anywhere.

"Go shower. If I'm hungry, I know you are," he stated before kissing my neck.

"Okay," I responded softly, not wanting to leave his warm embrace.

Strolling towards the bathroom, Jonzella's door opened as she sauntered out, wearing a pair of gray jogging pants and a white, spaghetti strapped shirt.

"Morning, sis," she yawned at the same time I said, "Hello."

"Morning?" Casey inquired quickly and then continued. "More like afternoon."

"Well damn," she replied as she spoke to him before asking, "Where is Totta?"

"Outside, smoking," he replied.

Caught Up in a D-Boy's Illest Love

"Oh, yeah, Jonsey, since your ass wouldn't answer the door this morning, I took the liberty to call your job and say that you were sick," she voiced as I tried to close the bathroom door.

Slapping my forehead, I forgot that I was scheduled to be to work at eight this morning.

"Well, damn. Thanks, Jonzella. How in the hell did I forget about going to work?"

"Dick was the reason why you forgot. Y'all damn near kept me and Totta up," she laughed until Casey said, "Now, you know that's a damn lie."

With Jonzella and Casey laughing at the true statement, I closed and locked the bathroom door before I disrobed. Turning on the shower, I slid off my robe while grabbing my toothbrush and the toothpaste. Stepping into the shower, I had a smile on my face as wide as the state of Texas. Who would've ever thought that I would find solace and confidence from Casey? Sure as hell not me. His soothing, sweet words about my appearance, the way I thought, etc. uplifted my once damaged pride. The thoughts of being humiliated by another male was lifted the moment Casey told me that he wasn't like the others and proved it.

Knock. Knock. Knock.

Caught Up in a D-Boy's Illest Love

"Please tell me you are almost done, Ms. Lady," Casey's deep voice stated.

"Not really, I'm just standing under the shower," I replied as the huge smile faded.

Damn, have I been in here too long? I thought at the same time he mumbled, "Okay."

"Let me hurry up so this man can eat," I told myself as I began to bathe my body.

Fifteen minutes later, I was dressed and strolling into the living room. On the sofa, Totta and Jonzella were eating. In the kitchen, Casey was placing grits on two plates.

Now, this is a man worth waiting for and having, I thought as I sauntered into the apple themed kitchen.

"What would you like to drink?" I asked upon opening the refrigerator door.

"I want you to have a seat, and I'll bring everything to you," he commanded as I pulled out the gallon of unopened orange juice.

"Nope. I'm going to help you," I said in a rebellious but nice tone.

Turning around to look at me, he shook his head and responded, "Why must you be so hardheaded?"

Caught Up in a D-Boy's Illest Love

"Same thing our parents ask," Jonzella stated before laughing.

Chuckling, I continued to help Casey. I was far from a lazy female. One thing I learned while growing up was that a woman helps her man, no matter the circumstances. In a relationship, it took two people to make things work. My parents have shown me that over the years, and I was going to take that knowledge and use it very well.

Finally sitting down to eat, Casey popped my hand right as I was about to shovel a spoonful of eggs and grits into my mouth. Immediately, Totta began to laugh. Looking at them both with a weird look on my face, Casey announced, "Grace first, and then we eat."

"Oohkay," I sounded off, awkwardly as I closed my eyes and bowed my head.

Casey said grace while Totta tried to stifle his laughter. Once grace was spoken, Casey and I began to eat. I was amazed that he was the religious type of being; given that at the redo date, we didn't say grace. Every day, I was learning something knew about the man that I secretly wanted for three years, and each time I grew more infatuated with him.

Caught Up in a D-Boy's Illest Love

An hour after we were done eating, the fellas went outside to smoke and talk. When they came back, they announced that they were leaving for the weekend. Jonzella said, "okay," whereas, I wanted to know where they were going and for how long. I was hoping that Jonzella was going to ask, but since she didn't, I politely asked.

"How long will you be gone, Casey, and where are you going?"

"I'm going to handle some business, and I'll be back Sunday night," he replied curtly.

Shocked at his tone, I nodded my head and said, "Be careful."

"Always," was his response before he went to my bedroom as Totta kissed Jonzella on the forehead and told her that he was going to get his shoes from her room.

Once they returned from our rooms, sensual kisses and hugs were given out. Shortly after, the fellas disappeared out of our home. I had a thousand questions that only Jonzella could answer.

"How often do they do this?"

"You mean handle business?" she asked quickly before answering my question, "Often. They leave at least two times a week," she replied calmly while looking at me.

"Well, got damn. What exactly do they do?"

"You already know the answer to that, Jonsey Marie Brown," she replied with a smirk on her face.

Chapter 15
Dank

Friday, January 6ᵗʰ, 2017
Evening

The ride to South Carolina would've been pleasurable, but the entire way Danzo, Totta, and I were on a business call with J-Money. We were negotiating ways to have him as a sharpshooter for what we need done. His only problem was what were we willing to do for him in return. Danzo and Totta looked at me since I was the one doing all the talking. I didn't want to be a part of a large organization such as The Savage Clique, but they did have great perks of being under them; however, like all the great illegal organizations, they will fall, and I didn't want to be a part of that. So, I told him that I would call him back once I got a better idea of how to return the favor to him.

Soon as we landed at a low-key hotel in North Charleston, which was minutes away from Myrtle Beach. The fellas and I began to collaborate on the ways to pay J-Money for his services. Rolling a blunt, Totta said, "We can either move some dope for him for a certain amount of time or just tell him that whatever favor he needs we are willing to do."

"I'm with Totta on this one. By any means, those fuck boys got to go. I'm not wearing a jumpsuit for no one," Danzo's husky voice spat.

"My thing is…I don't want to be known like that. I like the little system that we have. We making money, and we are low-key. I'm not trying to take over the world, be well-known, or have major clout like that. True enough, they have damn near every politician, police force, etc. on their team; however, they can still crumble. Ain't no one that fucking untouchable. Feel me?" I voiced seriously as I ran my left hand through my freshly cut hair.

"True. True," Totta replied quickly and then continued. "How about we get out here and camp the folks crib out? I'm sure we will come up with a way to return the favor."

"A'ight," Danzo and I replied in unison.

While I was cooking breakfast yesterday, Totta was in the dining area searching through the ladies' mail. He was looking for their parents' address. I didn't think he would find anything that their parents had sent them; on the contrary, he did. He didn't look at the contents inside of the envelope. He had gotten what he wanted, and he quickly typed it into his phone.

Thirty minutes later, we were at our destination. From the moment we pulled onto the girls' parents' neighborhood, I knew those people had massive bread. The community was elegant with manicured grass as several small heighted bushes were perfectly lined in front of the gray and brown large cemented rocks. Those same small bushes were also planted throughout the neighborhood. Houses were decorated with expensive pottery and brightly hued outside furniture. Not one home that we passed had a raggedy or beat up car in the driveway or on the curb. All the cars, I saw were no later than a 2015 model.

"What in the fuck do these chicks' folks do?" Danzo inquired in an amazed tone.

"Both parents are retired from the military," Totta and I stated at the same time.

"Ah, once again what in the fuck do their parents do? I know folks who been in the military and living like shit," Danzo stated in a matter-of-fact timbre.

"What are you implying, fool head?" Totta inquired before chuckling.

"Shit, mom and pops doing some illegal shit," he huffed.

As we patiently sat in the car waiting for them to show their faces, Danzo went on and on about Jonsey and Jonzella parents doing illegal activities. Totta and I were cracking up about his theory of them claiming to be wealthy from retiring from the military. There was no need in me educating the man on how they could've invested their money. Some folks always believed there were two ways to stay rich; selling drugs or having a million-dollar corporation.

Forty-five minutes into staking out the Brown's home, we saw the parents and the two snitches. Upon me seeing them, I knew what we had to do. Snatching up my phone, I called J-Money. On the second ring, he answered the phone.

"Speak to me, Dank," his deep southern voice stated.

"Whatever favor you want, we'll take care of that," I quickly told him as the burgundy car left the driveway.

"Where do you need me to be and when?" he questioned without a moment's hesitation.

"I'll let you know within the next hour or so."

"Bet," he replied, indicating that the conversation was over.

Caught Up in a D-Boy's Illest Love

Totta followed the Browns. We ended up in a shopping center, which had a grocery store, nail salon, pet place, and a gentleman's clothing store. The mother went into the nail salon as the guys went into a gentleman's store. Before disappearing into the store, the snitches seemed as if they were paranoid—they were looking over their shoulders every thirty seconds or so.

"What's the move? I'll pop their asses right here, on site," Danzo growled as he took his weapons off safety.

"We need to further surveillance them. I'm not sure if they should be knocked off up here or down in Alabama," I replied as I waited for them to come out of the store.

"Shid, the momma went into the nail shop...so, y'all know she gonna be in there for a minute," Totta stated causally before firing up a cigarette.

"I'll shoot off in there too. I prefer if all of them are dead. Hell, they could be the ones to send us to prison, too, if they know what their sons do," Danzo piped.

"Nawl, that's impossible. They weren't there. It's only he say, she say, even if they were to open their mouths," I voiced in an agitated tone.

We had already killed two people who we thought stole our shit and stashed it off. When in reality, Totta sold some packs and didn't tell me. I wasn't with killing people just to be killing them.

As we sat in the van waiting on them to return to their vehicles, I grew antsy. I was ready to get this shit over with. I had to make my promises to my grandmother and mother come true. Overall, a nigga was ready to continue his life just the way it was— single while a low-key dope dealer.

I didn't know how long my mind drifted off, but it was cut short upon hearing gunshots, multiple rounds. Most folks would duck down, but my ass was looking at the action. A black van with tinted windows had two mysterious niggas dressed in all-white with a white ski-mask pulled over their faces. Those guys held their weapons as if they were a part of the military, slanging bullets into their targets only. Zooming away from their position, on the ground were those two fuck niggas that snitched on us. A wide grin spread across my face as people inside of the stores came out. Totta and Danzo realized what happened to them, and they started clapping and saying, "That's what I'm talking 'bout. Handle that shit, nigga." Neither of us knew nor saw who shot those niggas.

Caught Up in a D-Boy's Illest Love

As Totta was starting to open his mouth, Jonsey's mother came out yelling, "Someone call 911," while running to her bleeding sons. Her husband wasn't in sight. Patrons of the stores slowly began to file out towards the scene. While we were sitting and watching things unfold, Totta and my phone sounded off. Quickly glancing at my screen, I saw Jonsey's name.

Before answering the phone, I told Danzo to be quiet and told Totta that we were just chilling—so that our story would match up. If I didn't tell Danzo to be quiet, he was liable to say something stupid.

"Ms. Lady, you must be thinking about me," I announced casually in the phone at the same time Totta voiced, "My girl, what's up?"

"I surely am," Jonsey cooed happily before giggling.

"I love that," I replied calmly as I looked at the crime scene with a smile on my black face.

"You better," she quickly stated before giggling.

Before I opened my mouth to respond with a smooth comment, Jonsey said, "So, when are you coming back?"

"Hopefully, tonight. A brother is kinda missing you."

"Kinda?" she shrieked as if her feelings were hurt.

Caught Up in a D-Boy's Illest Love

"Alright, alright, alright... a brother misses you quite a bit." I chuckled as I kept my eyes glued on the crime scene as the ambulance's sirens were blasting, which were soon in our eye sight.

"Now that is much better," she quickly said before she lowly spat, "Send me a dick pic."

Taken by surprise at her comment, I started coughing. As I tried to get my coughing under control, that heifer was laughing hard.

"You think that shit is funny, huh?" I questioned as Totta sat upright in the driver's seat and told Jonzella that he would call her back. That was my cue to end the call with Jonsey.

"Aye, Ms. Lady, I'mma have to call you back."

She groaned in disappointment but said okay. With our calls ended, I looked at Totta and was about to ask a question when Danzo yelped lowly, "Fuck, they ain't dead." Grinding his semi-yellow, uneven teeth together he began to breathe like a raging bull.

"It seems they aren't, but hopefully, they will be soon," Totta announced as he fired up another cigarette.

"Once they drive off, head back to the hotel. We'll watch the news later on tonight to see what they have to say. We'll make our decision on what to do based on if they are even breathing," I voiced blankly as I watched the fuck boys loaded into the ambulances.

"How 'bout y'all drop me off at the hospital, and I'll keep an eye on things," Danzo offered coolly.

Totta and I looked at each other and shook our heads. Having Danzo in the hospital would be an advantage that would be great for us. He knew how to be suave, helpful, and nosey. I just hoped that his ass didn't do anything stupid that would land us in prison.

***

At nine o'clock p.m., we were heading back to Alabama. With several blunts in the air and great feelings, Danzo, Totta, and I knew that things were on the up and up for us. Those fuck boys must've done something really crazy in South Carolina. Whoever wanted them dead came, visited the hospital, and tried to finish what they started.

From what Danzo told us, the hospital was placed on lockdown after both of the guys machines started going crazy. Immediately, I assumed that someone must've slipped something into their IV line, and I'll be damned if I wasn't right. Totta wanted to know where the parents were the entire time, and Danzo replied in the waiting area with him. Honestly, I didn't give a fuck where they were as long as their sons were dead.

I was glad when we touched back down in our state. I was in need of the one female that knew how to relax me. As I turned down the radio, I pulled out my cell phone and dialed Jonsey's number. While her phone rung, Totta was chuckling. I ignored his petty ass. On the fourth ring, she answered the phone, sleepily.

"Hello."

"You dreaming about me?" I inquired as I relaxed further into the passenger seat.

"Always. I'm missing you, Mr. Mosley."

"I'm missing you too, Ms. Lady. You want me to bring you something to eat?"

"No. Just come straight over."

"Okay. I'll be touching down within the next two hours or so."

"Okay."

"Get some rest, and I'll ring your phone soon as I'm outside of your crib."

"K." She yawned.

"That chick got you gon' man, just admit it," Totta joked as he briefly glanced at me.

Caught Up in a D-Boy's Illest Love

"Nawl, I just like her energy, and plus, she will give me the four-one-one on her brothers. That is the most important thing to me right now," I lied, looking out the window.

Waking up from a deep sleep, Danzo mumbled something, but we couldn't understand it.

"What?" We laughed at the hard sleeping fool in the back seat.

"We made it yet?"

"We in Alabama, but not The Gump," Totta stated as he passed a green Ford Focus.

"A'ight, drop me off at my crib," he mumbled lowly yet clearly.

"I know that, nigga." Totta chuckled as he mashed the gas pedal and turned up the radio.

With the radio's volume playing at a nice level, I drifted off into a world of my own. I thought about how good Jonsey was for me, and how good I was when I was with her. I didn't think about being in the streets. I honestly wanted to make an honest living with the degree that I had. A brother wanted a family and all, but I wanted to make sure that I had it with the right female. My worst fear was that things between Jonsey and I were just for now, and that she would change in the blink of an eye.

I was the type of dude that, when committed, I was only for that one person. I didn't entertain any other broads. Upfront bitches knew that I had a woman because I had mine in the limelight with me. I did what a man was supposed to do for his woman and home; however, I was not up for being taking for granted. That was the main reason why I tried to fuck and go on about my business because her persona had a nigga all in.

Ring. Ring. Ring.

Turning down the radio, Totta answered his phone.

"Yo," he piped lowly.

I knew immediately who was on the phone. His body language told me so. When Jonzella called, he was more relaxed and happy. A smile from here to Africa would be on his face as he read her name on his phone's screen.

"Heading back," he replied shortly after he answered the phone.

"I'll be there before you know it. Do you want anything to eat?" he asked softly.

I wasn't trying to eavesdrop or anything, but I had to joke on this nigga like he tried to do me.

"What is wrong with you?" he questioned seriously.

Caught Up in a D-Boy's Illest Love

"Shit, I'm sorry about your brothers, baby girl. Are they okay?" he asked sincerely as he pumped his right fist in the air.

"Take it easy, Ma. Pray about it. I'm on my way to you. Try not to stress. Things will work out for the best. Okay?"

Shortly after he hung up the phone, Totta looked at me and said, "Those fuck niggas in a coma. They don't know when or if they will ever make it out of it."

Chapter 16
Jonsey

Thursday, January 12th

Today was the first day that I was able to breathe since I learned of Kevin and Kenny being in a coma. Each day was harder to not be by their sides. Our parents told Jonzella and me to stay at school and focus. They were sure that our brothers would recover in excellent health.

A part of me knew that wasn't true. They had been in a coma for six days with minimal response. Whatever they had gotten into was surely coming back to haunt us instead of them. I wasn't ready to attend a double funeral, and I knew my parents weren't ready to bury two of their sons.

"Jonsey, what are you doing for the weekend?" one of my coworkers, Moneek asked, interrupting my thoughts, as I strolled to the breakroom.

"I'm going out of town with my sister and our guy friends," I voiced excitedly as I opened the rubbery, black double doors.

"Where to?"

Caught Up in a D-Boy's Illest Love

"Biloxi."

"Gambling?"

"Yeah."

"Damn, have fun for me. I'm stuck in Walmart everyday this weekend," she huffed.

"I surely will," I replied quickly.

I wasn't the type to carry a long conversation with Moneek; she was the messiest broad in the workplace. Placing my phone in my face, that was her cue to leave me the hell alone. In the notification bar, I saw an envelope—indicating that I had a text message.

Eager to see who sent me a message, I opened the icon. Not recognizing the number, I tapped the message. In the thread was a screenshot of a message thread. Completely lost at what I was looking at, I zoomed in so that I could read the message between the unknown persons.

After I realized what I read, with shaky hands, I rushed to dial Casey's number.

On the second ring, he sang, "My Queen."

"Fuck that my queen, shit. You think you going to be playing with my emotions is a damn lie. While you are up in my face, you out here telling a broad named Diamond that you love her. So, I'll tell you what,

Casey...you can lose my damn number because I'm not finna play these games. You got me once, but I be damned if you gon' get me twice," I voiced angrily before hanging the phone up in his face.

Stomping away from the break area, I didn't care that I had several coworkers looking at me, or all in my conversation. They were the least of my worries. I had to repair my hurt feelings. I had to figure out how was I going to get the dude I've daydreamed about for three years out of my system.

Ring. Ring. Ring.

Looking at my phone, I ignored Casey's call. The tears began to well in my eyes, causing me to slightly hold my head back so that they wouldn't fall. My phone rang again, and I ignored the call. After the seventh call from Casey, I placed his number on the block list.

Normally, I would've had a full-course meal for lunch, but after reading that screenshot message I didn't want to eat or drink anything. For my hour break, I sat in my car trying not to cry while I told Jonzella about the message. After being on the phone with her for five minutes, I had to hang the phone up in her face. She pissed me off with, "I told you to tread lightly with him anyways, Jonsey. You really haven't spent enough time with him to really know the guy." That was the last thing that I wanted to hear.

Upon clocking in and returning to the electronics department, I heard the familiar voice angrily spat, "Jonsey!"

I know damn well this nigga did not show up at my job, I thought as I made a sharp, right turn into my working space.

"Act like you didn't hear me calling you, guh!"

"Jonsey, please tell me you hear that fine ass dude calling your name," Frederick, or Fredericka as he liked to be called, stated in his fake girl voice.

"Yep. I hear him, and honestly I don't care," I replied as I aimed for the buggy that I sat in front of the five-dollar bin of movies while Casey was hollering my name.

Not responding to him, I finished my task of piling more movies into the reduced-price bin.

"Okay, so you gon' act like yo' ass don't hear me calling you," Casey voiced as he roughly turned me around.

"Don't touch me, dude!" I shrieked as I glared at him.

"You better stop yelling at me," he growled as he stepped closer in my face.

Slap!

Caught Up in a D-Boy's Illest Love

"Ohh, shit," Frederick/Fredericka and other coworkers sounded off after I slapped Casey.

With his right hand balled into a tight fist, his left hand grabbed me by my shirt.

Glaring into my eyes, he spat, "Don't you fuck with me. We had that established the first night. We need to discuss what was sent to you. Calm down so I can explain."

"Fuck you. Whatever we had going on is over!" I yelled as the tears streamed down my face.

"You gon' make me—," he began to say before he cut his words off as he released my shirt and unballed his fist.

"I'm at work. You need to leave. Whatever you have to say…you better tell Jesus because I gives no fucks!"

"You pissing me off, Jonsey."

"Go take that shit up with Diamond!" I yelled before turning around to finish my job before he messed around and got me fired.

Before I could wipe my face and sigh heavily, I was being lifted off the ground.

"What the fuck, Casey! Put me down!"

Caught Up in a D-Boy's Illest Love

"Hell no. Got me running around these folk's damn store, yelling your name and you can't answer me. Nawl, Jonsey...I'm carrying your ass out this doe!"

"Umm, sir, you need to leave the premises," Jasmine, one of the electronics department managers, demanded.

"I am...with Jonsey over my damn shoulders. All she had to do was listen to what I had to say...instead of putting on this damn show!"

"Casey, please put me down. This is my job. This is how I pay my freaking bills, dude," I voiced angrily. I was extremely embarrassed, and I wanted to be anywhere other than over his shoulders like a child.

"Guh, don't act like I don't have no fucking money. I'll pay your bills until you get another job...if I allow you to get another job. That's what a real man does when he causes his woman to lose her job," he announced loudly as he strolled away, aiming for the entrance/exit door of Walmart.

"Put me down. I can walk, you know."

Ignoring me, he kept on walking. Employees of Walmart, along with customers, were looking at us. All I could do was drop my bobbing ass head and close my eyes.

Caught Up in a D-Boy's Illest Love

This dude here already making me sick, I thought as the door greeter happily stated, "Have a great day."

"You have a great day as well," Casey replied as I didn't murmur a word.

On the way to his car, I quickly stated, "I'm not leaving my car here. I'm on row six. Take me to it!"

"Hand me your keys."

"They are in my right back pocket, Casey. Please put me down, my stomach is beginning to hurt," I whined as he dug in my pockets to retrieve my keys.

"I'm almost to my car. Totta, gonna drive your car back to your crib. I want your full attention from here on out, understand?"

I was severely pissed off; therefore, I didn't say anything. Two harsh pops to my bottom, I yelped, "Yes, Casey, I hear you…dang."

"Then respond when I'm talking to you," he loudly voiced as he planted me on the ground at the same time I heard Totta's voice.

"Manee, don't tell me you carried Jonsey out of her place of employment," Totta said while laughing.

"Yep, and embarrassed the hell out of me," I told him as I ambled towards the passenger's side of Casey's turquoise Infiniti.

Caught Up in a D-Boy's Illest Love

"You'll live, won't it?" he spat as I closed the door.

They talked briefly before Casey hopped in the front seat. While I looked out the window, I noticed his eyes on me. It seemed as time passed before he said anything.

"Diamond is an ex that won't get over me. We have been done for months. She came over to grab the rest of her belongings. We argued. She wanted to fight, and I had to hold my ground. She ended up with my phone. In the bathroom, she locked herself in with my phone. I kicked the door in to retrieve my phone and to kick her out of my house. End of story. That shit she sent you was a bunch of bullshit."

Pulling out my phone and opening the text message thread from ole girl, I handed him my phone.

"Read," I commanded, not looking at him.

Doing as he was told, that nigga began laughing. I didn't see shit funny.

"This hoe here needs to be stopped. Bitch had a whole conversation with herself. Jonsey, I have no reason to lie. I'm not fucking with that broad. Either you believe me or you don't."

"I choose to not believe you."

Caught Up in a D-Boy's Illest Love

"Okay," he announced angrily as he placed the gear shift in reverse.

Speeding away from Walmart's parking lot, I knew he was angry, and I didn't care one bit. He thought he had a gullible, dummy, but he was dead wrong. Just because I haven't been in many relationships, didn't mean a thing. Shit didn't smell right, and I wasn't going to stick around for it to plop on my face.

Casey was driving like a madman, and I loved my life. So, I had to tell him ease up off the gas.

"Umm, you do have a passenger in your car. You act like you want to have an accident on Ann Street. I'm not ready to die."

From my house to Walmart was approximately three minutes, there was no need to rush. That chocolate, gold mouth bastard was doing fifty in a thirty-five zone. I was damn near pissy once he made a sharp right turn on McQueen Street.

"Fuck, Casey! Chill out, seriously!" I yelled as my little body jerked left and then right.

Not saying a word, he flew down the street until he made a brief halt upon turning onto my street. When I say I was glad to be in my yard, I was thanking God for letting me live to see another minute. Totta was standing beside my car, shaking his head while laughing. As I hopped out of the passenger's seat, I asked for my keys.

Handing them to me, Casey spoke, "Jonsey, get that ass in the house. Totta, you can take my whip. I'm not leaving here no time soon. I'm sure you'll be back once Jonzella gets off."

I didn't hear the rest of their conversation since I ran to my room. I knew he was in the house because I heard the front door close, followed by the clinking of the locks.

"Where you at, Ms. Lady?" his sexy, deep voice timbre asked as he was in the front room.

"My room," I replied calmly.

As he strolled towards my vibrantly decorated room, Casey whistled. Upon reaching my door, he kicked off his all-black J's and waltzed towards me. With a smirk on my face, I shook my head and watched him take a seat next to me.

"Why are you shaking your head?" he asked.

"At the foolish things I be thinking and trying to accomplish."

"Like what?"

Caught Up in a D-Boy's Illest Love

"I know what you do...hence, me not asking you where you work. You are a trapper, and trappers can't be tamed no matter how good of a woman you are to them. I'm not what you are seeking, and I'm okay with that. I wanted you for so long that I never thought about competing with other females for you. Everything about you I liked from the way you dressed to how active you are in your mom and grandmother's lives. I guess I fell weak to the eleven golds in your mouth, your chocolate skin tone, and the fact that you read books," I stated before giving a weak chuckle and then continued, "At the end of the day, I can't be mad at you. You aren't my man, and I'm not your woman. So, either I'm going to play my role as the fuck buddy/homie or be done with the fantasy of having you as my man."

"Look—" he tried to say before I cut him off.

"Just go sit in the front room. Right now, I need some time to myself."

With his lips tightly closed, he nodded his head and stood up. Dropping my hands in my head, I began to talk some sense into myself. Halfway through my private, little pep talk, I was shoved on the bed as Casey parted my mouth with his tongue.

Caught Up in a D-Boy's Illest Love

"I ain't going nowhere, Jonsey. You don't have to worry about the next...'cause I'm yours," he mumbled inside of my mouth.

Wanting to break free from him, I couldn't. I was mushy in the man's hands that took my breath away whenever I saw him. Who could break away from that?

Chapter 17

Dank

Hearing Jonsey tell me how she felt did something to my heart. For her to say that she was willing to play her part just to be with me, gave me the go ahead to please and bless her body. Her speech made me realize that she was the one for me, and I had to put my guard down.

However, I couldn't put it too far down—granted that her brothers were still on our kill list. A ninja was at a crossroads with his feelings, and I didn't know what to do other than keep her legs open as I slowly rocked her body.

"Aye, Dank, we hitting the streets for a while tonight?" Totta inquired, interrupting my thoughts, upon seeing me in the kitchen.

"Yeah," I replied as I poured milk in a cup for Jonsey and juice in a cup for me.

"A'ight. Jonzella's ass is knocked out. What about Jonsey?"

"She close to it." I yawned.

"Hell, it looks like you are too," he laughed.

"Mane, that girl gon' fuck around and get got...I swear."

"I wouldn't be surprised if Jonzella hit me with the 'I'm pregnant' shit some weeks down the road from here."

"You skinny dipping, already?" I asked awkwardly while shaking my head.

"Truth be told, manne, I been kicking it with Jonzella. Three weeks ago, the condom broke, and I said to hell with it. I been skinny dipping ever since. She got a job. I'm a hustler. Shid, my seed gonna be straight," he stated seriously.

I noticed as he told his truth there was a brief flicker of happiness in his eyes; I knew that it was some serious shit behind it. Totta was falling for Jonzella, and I didn't blame him. She was a beautiful, smart, and fun woman. She was like Jonsey but not so much as shy. They were good women. The only problem was that we weren't good enough for them.

"Whatever you do...keep your head in the game. We gotta come out on top," I whispered to him.

"Always, man, always."

Strolling away from the kitchen, Totta let out a long, harsh sigh. I recognized that sound because I had released it every time I thought about the shit we were going to do to Jonzella and Jonsey's family—destroy it. If I could turn back the hands of time, I would just to spare their feelings; however, since I couldn't, I had to live with what Totta and I had to do.

***

"Quick in and out," Totta informed Tron.

"Nawl, I'm on chill mode," he said before laughing and hopping out of Totta's whip.

Stepping inside of Club Freeze, we handled our business, followed by chilling in the background. The club wasn't popping worth a damn. My thoughts dropped on Jonsey and that beautiful smile of hers, which quickly brought a smile to my face. That was until Totta shoved his brightly lit up phone to my face. I watched a good amount of the video he was showing me before it dawned on me who I was watching.

Pushing the phone out of my face, I stormed out of the club. Bitches were trying to hug me, and I shoved them out of the way. No need to see if Totta was behind me because if I was mad, he was equally pissed off.

Soon as we stepped out the doors, he yelled, "I'm going to fuck her ass into a coma! I told her not to bring her ass out this damn doe. I swear her ass is hardheaded.

Dank, if she hollers for help...I ain't hurting her just putting this dick on her. You, nor Jonsey, don't come save her from this dick punishment."

"Woe, now you know damn well, I'm finna blitz Jonsey's ass. Where the fuck they at?"

"Club Magic."

Grinding my teeth together, I was eager to get to the most ratchet club in the city. There was no way I was going to have Jonsey in that type of atmosphere, knowing how those niggas got down. Hopping in Totta's whip, I had to break the ice on our actions towards them.

"Mane, what in the fuck are we really doing with these girls? We trying to off their brothers, but it seems like we falling head over heels for them."

Sighing heavily as he backed out of the parking spot, Totta calmly spoke, "Mane, I ain't gon' lie like I don't have feelings for Jonzella. I didn't want to admit it, but it's true. Hands down, she got a hold on a nigga."

"Can you kill her brothers, and be at their funerals all the while consoling her?" I asked curiously.

"Be crying and all like I got love for them niggas," he laughed while beating on the wheel.

"Dude, you sick as fuck," I voiced as I shook my head.

"What about you?" his thick timbre inquired.

"It would hurt me for real to see Jonsey or Jonzella grieving over their family members. I don't think I can be around Jonsey knowing that I am solely the reason why she is in pain."

"Look at it this way, either be in prison for life without them or be free with them while they are grieving over their useless brothers...which the grieving won't last too long. A year at the least."

Sitting back and thinking while he drove like a mad man the short distance to Club Magic, I thought about what he said. Totta was a hardcore guy, but he did make sense. We were alike in a lot of ways, and other ways we weren't; this task was clearly not an easy one for me. I was constantly bouncing between whether or not to hurt Jonsey in such a harsh manner. Whenever she talked about her brothers, there was this undeniable love for them. She admired her siblings, even though two of them didn't do anything for her to admire.

My thoughts ceased soon as Totta's vehicle stopped in front of Club Magic. Turning off the engine, we stepped out and talked to one of the security guards. They quickly patted us down before granting us access to the club. Not wasting anytime, we strolled towards the DJ's booth. Totta paid the man to cut the music off and hand him the microphone.

"This is a public service announcement...umm, it's two hard headed women in this club by the names of Jonzella Brown and Jonsey Brown. Y'all got fourteen seconds to get out of this club."

We didn't see any movement; therefore, I hopped on the mic.

"I swear, Jonsey...whatever you trying to pull...I promise you gon' regret it...I told you don't fuck with me! Get that ass to Totta's truck, now!"

In the back of the club by the picture booth, I heard her say, "Get cho' black ass off that stage, and let's go home!"

With a smile on our faces, we thanked the DJ before handing him the mic. Jonsey and Jonzella was dolled up, and I knew for sure that they had niggas' attention, which quickly took the smile off my face. Quickly walking out of the club, we ran into them as they were heavily pissed off.

"I don't know why y'all are trying to be our daddies...we already have one. In case y'all forgot?" my slick mouthed woman said while Jonzella kept her eyes on Totta.

Caught Up in a D-Boy's Illest Love

"Casey, you know I'm feeling sour towards you right now," Jonsey slick mouthed ass continued.

I knew she was still heated from Diamond texting her, but once I got in her guts that attitude changed. The attitude reappeared as soon as we both climaxed. I had to find a way to let her know that I meant business and that there wasn't anyone else that I was entertaining. The only way I knew to do that was play the reverse psychology shit.

"You know what...you are right. You do have a daddy. I'll let you be, Jonsey. I'll give you your breathing space. You got my number whenever you want to call," I stated calmly before walking towards Totta's truck.

I knew she was expecting for me to embarrass her like I did earlier at her job. God knows I wanted to lift her petite body over my shoulders and place her in the backseat.

"Jonzella, you don't get off. You better fly to whomever whip y'all rode in. I swear you are in so much trouble right now, you wouldn't believe how much," I heard Totta say through clenched teeth.

"Okay," she obediently replied before walking away.

Caught Up in a D-Boy's Illest Love

"I know damn well you ain't letting Totta tell you what to do. You ain't never listen to what no nigga told you. You grown, remember?" Jonsey voiced angrily.

Coming to a complete stop and looking at her sister, Jonzella replied calmly, "Yes, I am grown Jonsey, and no I didn't let any nigga tell me what to do. However, Totta is not a just an ordinary nigga. Totta's my man. What Zaddy says goes."

Jonzella's cool snap back was so severe that all Jonsey could do was follow behind her. I looked at Totta, and he was smiling from ear to ear. I had to know what he did to get Jonzella in compliance. I was catching hell getting Jonsey on the right path, but then again, Diamond's funky ass messed that up.

Totta stood outside of his truck until he saw Jonzella's blue Nissan Altima pull off. Hopping in his whip, he started the engine, and sped behind our women. The entire trip, I was hoping that Jonsey was going to call me. She never did, and it hurt my feelings.

"Are you coming over anyways?" Totta inquired as he turned on McQueen Street.

"Nawl, I'm going to head home. You can drop me off at the edge of Dewenee Street. I'll walk to my car."

Caught Up in a D-Boy's Illest Love

"Are you sure?" he probed as he brought his Yukon to a stop.

"Yeah. I'm going to give her some space. Maybe I need space also. I gotta figure out a clear way to get out of this jam that we are in without hurting their souls."

"Just don't worry about them hurting over some fuck niggas' lives. They will recover with us by their sides, man."

"It's easy for you to deceive Jonzella like that. I can't be in Jonsey's face knowing that I'm the reason she's hurting."

"Whatever you choose, just make sure that we are not in prison. You know what I'm going to do if they aren't dead...off them niggas."

"Have she told you anything else about them?"

"Nope."

"Have you even inquired about them?"

"Yeah. All she says is that they are still in a coma, and the doctors not sure when they will come out of it or if they ever come out."

"That's great news honestly. Well, have a good night, woe."

"You do the same."

Caught Up in a D-Boy's Illest Love

Before hopping out, we dapped each other up. Once he pulled off, I texted Jonsey goodnight. I was hoping that she was going to text me back quickly, but that stubborn woman didn't. I couldn't lie like that shit didn't make me mad. I wanted to pop up at her house and demand that she talked to me, but I decided that it was best to go home and give her space.

Halfway to my home, my phone rang. Quickly looking down to see Jonsey displaying across my screen, I slid my thumb across the ignore option. As bad as I wanted to converse with her, I knew it was in our best interest to not be around each other for a couple of days. I needed to find out what I wanted between the two of us. There were decisions to be made, and I didn't want to make the wrong one that could hurt her. Planning to off her brothers was already hanging in the air.

Ring. Ring. Ring.

Dropping my head to take a quick glance at my phone, I snatched it up and answered it.

"Hello."

"Are you alright, son?" my mother voiced in a concerned tone.

"Yes, ma'am. Why do you ask that?" I replied as I turned onto Fifth Street.

"I saw you sitting in your car before you pulled off. I just wanted to make sure that you were okay."

"I am."

"You know I'm here for you if you ever want to talk."

"I know."

"Is it about a girl?" she continued to probe.

"Mama, I'm fine." I lied.

"I swear you are not as convincing as you think you are, Casey. Tomorrow, you will tell me exactly who this woman is that have your boxers in a bunch."

Shaking my head as I turned off the engine, I said, "Okay. How's brunch at Wintzell's sound?"

"Like a wonderful idea. Shall I tell your grandmother about our brunch date?"

"Yes," I chuckled, knowing that I was going to have one helluva time with those two women.

"You talked to your father, lately?"

"I talked to him two weeks ago. He's still pissed at me."

"He will come around. Just keep being the loving son that you are. He'll forgive you. If he chooses not to, then that will be on him."

Nodding my head, I stated, "Mama, it's late. Go to bed, and I'll be there to pick you and Grandma up around eleven o'clock. Please and I mean *please* be ready. Oh, tell grandma don't put on all that White Diamond mess. It's allergy season."

My mother had a hearty laugh before responding, "I'm going to make sure I tell her. You know she is going to cuss you out."

"I know," I yawned.

"Well, I won't keep you any longer. Goodnight, son."

"Goodnight, Mama. I love you."

"I love you more."

Hanging up the phone, I was grateful to have two women as loving and caring as my mother and grandmother. If no one in this world had my back, Gloria and Geraldine had it. Since I came into this world, them and my father were always there nurturing and telling me right from wrong. Of course, I didn't want for anything, but it felt like I was missing something; thus, I hit the streets and fell in love with it. I wasn't a big-time dope boy, yet I wasn't a small one either. I never worked a day in my life, which was my choice.

I graduated from high school with honors courses under my belt. Scholarships for college, I had that. If I hadn't graduated from high school, I wouldn't be alive today because my parents and grandmother would've whooped me to death. Graduation from college, I did that. I had a Bachelor's Degree in Engineering. With the types of knowledge that I possessed, I knew that I didn't want to work for anyone but myself.

That's when my dad, Curtis Price, and I fell out. He didn't like that I preferred the streets over a paycheck, and I was okay with his opinion. At the end of the day, I was a grown man, living on my own, no kids, and didn't ask anyone could I borrow anything. I paid for what I wanted no matter the cost!

My dad and mother were once married. They went their separate ways once I turned thirteen. I never understood why they decided that they weren't in love anymore. It was odd how I grew up with two loving parents in the home, and before I hit puberty good enough, my mother and I were moving back to Alabama.

It was a bittersweet move back to my mother's native state. I was so used to being around my dad that I hated them for a while. He was the only man that I had been around since I came into the world. Every time I thought about us not living in Texas as a family together, the further I jumped in the streets.

Ring. Ring. Ring.

I was glad that my phone began to ring so that I could stop thinking about my past. Every time I dipped into the past, sour feelings rose heavily within me and it took days for it to leave me.

Glancing down at my phone, I saw Jonsey's name on the screen and thought, *Oh, now her little ass wanna talk.*

Not wanting to talk to her, I ignored the call. Seconds later she called me back, and I ignored it again. Then my phone started chiming—back to back to back, text messages. I opened the first one to see what she had to say in all caps it read.

Jonsey: YOU MUST BE WITH THAT BITCH DIAMOND...SO I TELL YOU THE FUCK WHAT DON'T COME BY MY HOUSE OR JOB. DON'T RING THIS LINE! YOU FULL OF SHIT, AND I KNEW I SHOULD'VE STAYED AWAY FROM YOUR HOOD ASS WHEN YOU MADE A THOUSAND DOLLAR BET TO FUCK ME!

I didn't read the other text messages she sent before I started the engine on my whip. Quickly reversing out of my yard, I zoomed to Jonsey's house. One thing I knew, Jonsey was going to learn to stop playing with me. A nigga had too many emotions flooding through him to be dealing with the foolery for her. She had to learn that what I said goes. A nigga didn't want anyone but her. I could barely eat for thinking about her. When her name is mentioned, I damn near stop breathing.

As I thought about my crazy lady, I made it to her house within five minutes. What we weren't going to do was tongue wrestle with each other; well, not in the manner where we would be talking. After I closed my door, I jogged to the front door and rang the doorbell.

"Who is it?" Jonsey's soft voice asked before opening the door.

"Casey."

Slowly unlocking the door, she finally opened it. I wanted to be mad at how she came to the door, but my dick and eyes couldn't.

"Are you planning on coming in, or are you going to stand there and ogle me?" she inquired sassily as she placed her hands on her exposed hips while rolling her eyes.

"It's not just you and Jonzella in the house, so why are you walking around in a sport's bra and boy shorts?" I asked as I stepped across the threshold, followed by closing the door behind me.

Laughing, she replied, "Now you know dang well they are not coming out of the room no time soon. She's in trouble. In case you didn't notice, music is playing from her room."

"She ain't the only one in trouble...get to your room now!"

"Nope...is your little quickie over with? She can't fuck you like I do, huh?" she asked nastily before walking away.

Snatching her to me, I whispered in her ear, "No one has ever sucked or fucked me like you do. Jonsey, I'm feeling something for you that I shouldn't be. It's too early for that, and I know it. I wanted to fuck you once and drop you like a bad habit, but a nigga couldn't do that. I've looked for reasons to stop contacting and being around you, and for the life of me, I couldn't come up with a single thing. There is no one that I'm sleeping with...it's just you, Jonsey. I am not the controlling type, and I'll never be that. However, I do know how the streets are; thus, me telling you not to go here or there because I know what could happen to you." There was so much that I wanted to say, but I left it lingering in my brain, and honestly, that was a good thing for Totta and me.

Turning around to face me, Jonsey's watery eyes glared into my dry peepers. We stared at each other for a while before I secured her legs around my waist. While I strolled us along to her room, she brought her head closer to mine as I brought mine to hers. Licking her lips, I sneakily slid my tongue into her warm, wet mouth. Reciprocating the sensual kiss that I was giving her, Jonsey went the extra mile to massage my head while sucking on my tongue. Lord knows that I enjoyed every touch, kiss, stroke, or whatever she did to my body to the point that I wished her brothers would die soon! Every fiber in me wanted us to be together for the rest of our natural lives.

"I don't want to fuck or sex tonight, Jonsey...I wanna make love to you," I groaned in her mouth as I closed her bedroom door with the heel of my right foot.

"I don't know how to do that," she stated shyly.

"You do it to me every time I climb in between your legs," I voiced sweetly as I placed her gently on the bed.

The magic in her bedroom took off soon as I decided that I wasn't going to use a condom. That could've been the worst mistake that I made, but I did what my heart commanded.

Chapter 18

Jonsey

Friday, January 13th

Boy, what a late night/early morning I had with Casey. Several times, I had to pinch myself to see if it was real. When the sun came up, Casey was still wide awake as he pleased me. I had to tell him that I had to go to sleep, but his stubborn tail wouldn't give my body a break. When he said that he didn't want to fuck or sex me, he meant it. Nothing but slow grinding until thirty minutes ago.

"Set your alarm for an hour; once it goes off, get up and get dressed. Don't oversleep, Ms. Lady. I'm going to have brunch with my mama and grandmother. When I come back we are heading to Biloxi," he voiced as he planted a kiss on my neck.

"So, you telling me that after the late night/early morning that we just had...you want to get on the road?" I asked in an astonished tone.

"Yep. Totta and Jonzella been sleep, so they can do the driving," he replied as he slipped his shoes on.

"Okay. Be safe," I yawned as I snuggled my naked body back in my bed.

Caught Up in a D-Boy's Illest Love

Before leaving my room, he gave me a deep, sensual kiss. Seeing a huge smile on his face before he turned around made my heart flutter.

Before closing the door behind him, Casey said, "Set that alarm clock, Jonsey."

"Okay," I yawned as I closed my eyes.

My damn eyes weren't shut a good minute before Jonzella sashayed her loud mouth tail in my room.

"Ain't no sleeping on this beautiful Friday. We have a trip to get ready forrrr!"

"Now, Jonzella, why must you be so loud? Damn," I yelped in an agitated timbre as I glared at her angrily.

"Well, you should've told Casey to get off you so that you could go to sleep. Get up…I want to get my nails, toes, eyelashes, and eyebrows done," she excitedly voiced, hopping into my bed.

"Why can't you go natural for one week, Jonzella?"

"Umm, we are going out of town. Get up and stop asking all of these questions."

"I'm tirreed."

"Not my problem," she hissed as she threw the covers off me.

Ring. Ring. Ring.

"Whyyy?" I cried out as my cell phone rang.

Caught Up in a D-Boy's Illest Love

Snatching it from my nightstand, our mother's name displayed across the screen. A long sigh escaped my lips and Jonzella said, "Girl, answer the phone for Mommy."

Nodding my head, I slid my finger across the answer option followed by placing the call on speakerphone.

"Hello," Jonzella sang as I said it rather sloppily.

"Well, hello my lovely daughters. What are you guys up to on the beautiful Friday?"

"We are getting ready for our trip to Biloxi. What are you doing?" Jonzella's big mouth blurted. I wanted to slap her face off. Our mother was the last person that I needed to know where we were going.

"With who, ladies? I want their full names, licenses plate, the name of the hotel y'all will be staying in, and what everyone is wearing. There will be no drinking and driving. Get condoms because I do not want any grandchildren from you two right now. Do not be texting and talking on the phones. Y'all better behave down there. Hold on for a second...Roberrrtt!" our mother yelled, calling for our father.

My angry face had Jonzella giggling. I made sure to tell her that I was extremely pissed for her telling Mom that we were going somewhere. Every time we decided to go anywhere, our mother did the damn most. She wanted too much information. I thanked God that she was not in the same city as us because she would have pulled up to take pictures of us, the cars, licenses plates, and anything else she thought would help the police find us—if we ever went missing.

"Sweeties, how are y'all?" our father asked as he chewed on something.

"Great, Daddy," we responded in unison.

"Your mother and I are coming down to visit you guys in two weeks."

"Yaay," Jonzella spat happily at the same time I said, "For how long?"

"For four days. We have to talk to some important people. Your knuckleheaded brothers don' got themselves into some mess before they were shot, and we have to take care of it," our father spoke. There was no reason for Jonzella or me to ask which brothers because we already knew—Kenny and Kevin.

"What have they gotten into now?" Jonzella inquired as she shook her head with a smirk on her face.

Immediately, I turned down the volume on my phone. Our mother's voice was very loud, and I didn't want our brothers' business to be heard by Totta.

Caught Up in a D-Boy's Illest Love

"They were present when two guys, who are dead now, were held hostage in a house. The last time the guys were seen alive was when they were in the house with three men and your brothers. So, your brothers are witnesses as to who were the last people to see those guys alive," our mother stated in a low tone.

"Why didn't we know about this?" Jonzella voiced, angrily.

"Because we didn't want to put you two in harm's way," our mother responded sincerely.

"How would we be in any danger? How important are Kenny and Kevin if they are in a coma now?" I inquired curiously.

"Because Jonzella's bullheaded ass would be trying to help the prosecuting team get those thugs off the streets. That's why we are coming down to talk to your brothers' lawyer and the law enforcement team to see what is going to be done since they are in a coma," our mother announced in a matter-of-fact tone.

"If Kenny and Kevin saw those guys, and identified them...y'all know who the guys are, right?" Jonzella said quietly.

"Yep," they replied in unison.

Caught Up in a D-Boy's Illest Love

"Who?" we questioned in unison as we looked at each other.

"Joshua Nixon aka Totta and Casey Moseley aka Dank," my father spat at the same time Jonzella passed out.................

Caught Up in a D-Boy's Illest Love

TN Jones was born in Montgomery, Alabama but raised in Prattville, Alabama. She currently resides in Montgomery, Alabama with her boyfriend and their daughter. Growing up, TN Jones always had a passion for reading and writing. She began writing short stories when she was a young teen but didn't take her craft seriously.

As a college student, TN Jones enjoyed writing academic research papers which made her believe that she was choosing the wrong career path in Business and Management. After a bilateral axilla and inguinal surgery in 2015, she started working on her first book.

TN Jones does not have a set genre she writes in. She will write in the following genres: Contemporary fiction, Urban fiction, Mystery/Suspense, Interracial/Urban Romance, Dark Erotica, and Fantasy fiction novels.

Published novels by TN Jones: *Disloyal: Revenge of a Broken Heart, Disloyal 2: A Woman's Revenge, Disloyal 3: A Woman's Revenge, A Sucka in Love for a Thug, If You'll Give Me Your Heart, If You'll Give Me Your Heart 2: All or Nothing, By Any Means: Going Against the Grain* series, & *The Sins of Love: Finessing the Enemies 1-2.*

Caught Up in a D-Boy's Illest Love

Thank you for reading part one of *Caught Up In A D-Boy's Illest Love*. Please leave an honest review under the book title on Amazon's page.